Christabel Coleridge

An English squire :

A novel

Christabel Coleridge

An English squire :
A novel

ISBN/EAN: 9783337101060

Printed in Europe, USA, Canada, Australia, Japan

Cover: Foto ©Andreas Hilbeck / pixelio.de

More available books at **www.hansebooks.com**

AN ENGLISH SQUIRE.

A Novel.

BY

C. R. COLERIDGE,

AUTHOR OF "LADY BETTY," "HANBURY MILLS," "HUGH CRICHTON'S ROMANCE," ETC.

IN THREE VOLUMES.

VOL. II.

AIM HIGH, STRIKE HIGH.

London :

SAMPSON LOW, MARSTON, SEARLE, & RIVINGTON,

CROWN BUILDINGS, 188, FLEET STREET.

1881.

CONTENTS.

Part III.—Seville.

PART II.

BROTHERS.

"There are none so dependent on the kindness of others
as those that are exuberantly kind themselves."

AN ENGLISH SQUIRE.

CHAPTER XIX.

LIFE AND DEATH.

" As we descended, following hope,
  There sat the shadow feared of man."

PERHAPS it was well for the permanence
of Cheriton's new-born happiness that he
had but a very short glimpse of Ruth.
The next morning, the Oakby party
started early, that Mr. Lester might
arrive in time to attend a magistrate's
meeting at Hazelby, while Ruth remained
for the later train that was to take her on
her separate visit. She would not give him
a chance of seeing her alone, and one look,
one clasp of the hand, and—" Remember
your promise " was all the satisfaction he

B 2

obtained from her. Yet he could hardly
collect his thoughts to answer his father's
many questions on their journey home,
and trying to shout through the noise of
the train made him cough so much that
his grandmother scolded him for catching
such a bad cold.

" Young men are so foolish," she said,
but she did not look at all uneasy. *Her*
grandchildren's illnesses were never
serious; and all the Lesters thought any
amount of discomfort preferable to " having a fuss made." Cherry hardly knew
himself how ill he was feeling, as they
reached home and the day went on; but
he was so weary with bad nights and
fatigue that it was a perpetual effort to
remember that all his suspense of every
sort was over, that the examination was
passed, and that Ruth was his. He lay
on the sofa trying to rest; but the cough
disturbed him, and by dinner-time he was
obliged to own himself beaten and to go
to bed, saying that a night's rest would
quite set him up again.

"Boys have no moderation," said Mr. Lester, in a tone of annoyance. "It is well it is all over now. Cheriton might have taken quite as good a place without overworking himself in this way."

Alvar, not understanding that peculiarly English form of anxiety that shows itself in shortness of temper, thought this remark very unfeeling. Mrs. Lester suggested some simple remedy for the cough; Cherry promised to try it, and was left to his "night's rest."

He woke in the early morning from a short, feverish sleep, to such pain and breathlessness and such a sense of serious illness as he had never experienced in his life, and, thoroughly frightened and bewildered, was trying to think how he could call any one, when his door was softly opened, and Alvar came in.

"I heard you cough so much," he said. "You cannot sleep. I am afraid you are ill."

"Very ill," said Cherry. "You must send some one for the doctor."

He was but just able to tell Alvar
where to find the young groom who could
ride into Hazelby to fetch him; and soon
there was terrible alarm through all
the prosperous household, as, roused one
after another, they came to see what was
amiss. Nettie fled, with her hands up to
her ears, right out into the dewy garden,
away from the house, afraid to hear what
the doctor said of Cherry. Mr. Lester
gave vent to one outburst of rage with
examiners, examination, and Oxford generally, then braced himself to wait in
silence for tidings; as he had waited once
before when his wife lay in mortal danger
—would the verdict be the same now?
Mrs. Lester preserved her self-possession,
sent for the keeper's wife, who was the
best nurse at hand, and though sadly at
a loss what remedies to suggest, sat
down to watch her grandson, because it
was her place to do so.

They were all too thankful for any help
in the crisis to wonder that it was Alvar
who held Cherry in an easier position,
and soothed him with quiet tenderness.

When the doctor at length arrived, he pronounced that Cheriton was suffering from a violent attack of inflammation of the lungs. He was very ill; but his youth and previous good health were in his favour. Overwork and the neglected cold would doubtless account for it.

"Will it be over—in a fortnight?" said Cherry, suddenly.

"We'll hope so—we'll hope so," said the doctor. "You have only to do as you are told, you know. Now, have you a good nurse?" turning to Mrs. Lester.

"Yes, we think Mrs. Thornton very trustworthy—she was nursery-maid here before she married."

"There must be as few people about him as possible. No talking and no excitement."

"But—Alvar will stay?" said Cherry, wistfully. "Father, he came in the night —I want him."

"Hush, hush, my boy—yes, of course he will stay with you if you like," said Mr. Lester, hastily.

"Of course," said Alvar, with a curious

accent, half proud, half tender, as he laid his hand on Cheriton's.

The foreign brother was the last person whom Mr. Adamson expected to see in such a capacity ; but if he was inefficient, both he and his patient would probably soon discover it ; he looked the most self-possessed of the party, and his manner soothed Cheriton. Mrs. Thornton had plenty of practical experience to supply his inevitable ignorance. Cheriton was exceedingly ill; his strength did not hold out against the remedies as well as had been hoped, and he suffered so much as to be hardly ever clearly conscious.

"I was so happy!" he said several times with a sort of wonder, and his father felt that the words gave him another pang.

Mr. Lester was threatened with the most terrible sorrow that could befall him, and no mitigation of the agony was possible to him. He thought that his best-loved son would die, and made up his mind to the worst, feeling hope impossible ; but he made a conscientious effort at endurance, an effort sadly unsuccessful.

"Eh! my son," said his old mother, "he is a good lad, take that comfort."

And this reserved hint at the one real consolation was almost the only attempt at comforting each other that any of them made. No one tried to "make the best of it," to look at the hopeful side, or to find in any mutual tenderness a little lightening of the burden. They held apart from each other with a curious shyness, and as far as possible pursued their several businesses. Nettie went to her lessons, and refused to hear a word of sympathy from her friends, and when at last she could endure the agony no longer, ran away by herself into the woods and hid herself all day. Why should they kiss her and give her flowers—it did not cure Cherry, or make it less dreadful that another doctor was coming from Edinburgh, because Mr. Adamson thought him so ill. But she did not want to see him, and had no instinct whatever to do any-

thing for him. Speech was no relief to
any of them; it was easier to conceal than
to indulge their feelings; and Mr. Lester
went about silent and stern; Nettie attempted to comfort no one but the dogs;
and her grandmother found no relief but
in talking of Cherry's "folly in overworking himself" to Virginia, who came
hurriedly at the first report that reached
Elderthwaite. She was a rare visitor; it
was characteristic of her relations with
Alvar that a sort of shyness kept her
away. She forgot to be shy, however,
when Alvar came to speak to her for a
moment, and sprang towards him.

"Oh! dear Alvar, this is terrible. I
am so sorry for you. But you think he
will be better."

"Yes, surely," said Alvar, as if no other
view had occurred to him. "*Mi dona*,
this is wrong that I should let you seek
me; but I cannot leave him—he suffers so
much—that cough is frightful."

"But he likes to have you with him?'

"Yes, I can lift him best, and I do not

ask him how he is when he cannot speak,"
said Alvar, with the simplicity that was so
like sarcasm. " Ah ! it is not right to
let you go back alone, *mi Reyna*—but I
dare not stay."

" That does not matter; only take care
of yourself," said Virginia, as Alvar kissed
her hand and opened the door for her, and
promised to let her have news every day.

But she went away tearful for more than
Cheriton's danger. Alvar had never told
her that it comforted him to see her; he
did not care whether she came or not.

" Eh ! my lass, what news have you ? "
said an anxious voice, and looking up,
Virginia saw her uncle, looking unusually
clerical for a week day, hanging about the
path in front of her.

" Alvar thinks he will be better, he is
very ill now," said Virginia; " they have
sent for another doctor."

" Ah ! that's bad ! There's never been
such another in all the country. Queenie,
did I ever tell you how he kept up our
credit with the bishop ? "

And Parson Seyton, whose nature was very different from his neighbour's, spent a long hour in telling tales of Cherry's boyhood to his willing listener. "Eh!" he concluded, "and I meant to fetch him over to hear our fine singing, and see how spick and span we are now-a-days—new surplice and all! Eh! he wrote me a sermon once—when he was a little lad not twelve years old—and I'll swear it might have been preached with the best."

Although Virginia had said nothing and done little to mend matters at Elderthwaite, there had been a certain revival of the elements of respectability. A drunken old farmer had been succeeded by his son, who had been brought up and had married elsewhere. This young couple came to church, and Virginia had by chance made acquaintance with the bride. Her husband got himself made churchwarden—Elderthwaite was not enlightened enough for parochial contests, and Virginia having shyly intimated that want of means need not stand in the way, the windows were

mended, and some yards of cocoa-nut mat-
ting appeared in the aisle. There had
always been a little forlorn singing; young
Mr. and Mrs. Clement were musical, and
the Sunday children were collected in the
week and taught to sing. The parson had
been presented with the surplice, and as by
this time he would have done most things
to please his pretty niece, accepted it with
some pride. Whether from the effect of
these splendours, or from consideration for
the fair attentive face that he never failed
to see before him, the parson himself began
to conduct the service with a slight regard
to decency and order; and being with his
Seyton sense of humour fully conscious of
the improvement, and, with the simplicity
that was like a grain of salt in his character, rather proud of it, had looked forward
to Cherry's approbation.

"Eh!" he said, "I'd like to see him—
I'd like to see him."

"He mustn't see any one," said Virginia; "they will hardly let his father go
in."

" Well, it's a pity it's not the Frenchman.   Eh! bless my soul, my darling, I
forgot."

"Alvar is almost ready to think so too,
uncle," said Virginia, hardly able to help
laughing.

" If I could do anything that he would
like—catch him some trout—" suggested
the parson.

"Uncle," said Virginia timidly, "in
church, when any one is sick or in trouble,
they pray for them. They will mention
Cherry's name at Oakby to-morrow. Could
not we—"

" Ay, my lass, it would show a very proper respect," said the parson; "and the
lad would like it too."

And of all the many hearty prayers that
were sent up on that Sunday for Cheriton
Lester's recovery, none were more sincere
than rough Parson Seyton's.

The Edinburgh doctor could only tell
them what they knew before, that though
there was very great danger, the case was
not hopeless. A few days must decide it.

In the meantime he must not talk—he must not see any one who would cause the slightest agitation; and poor Mr. Lester, whose self-control had suddenly broken down before the interview, was about to be peremptorily banished; but Cherry put out his hand and caught his father's, looking up in his face.

"Send for the boys," he said.

"Yes, but you know you mustn't see them, my boy—my dear boy."

"But Cherry will like to know they are here," said Alvar, in the steady voice that always seemed like a support.

"They shall come. What else—what is it, Cherry?" said Mr. Lester, as his son still gazed at him wistfully.

"Nothing—not *yet*," whispered Cheriton. "Oh! I want to say so much, father! I am so glad Alvar came home!"

The words and the sort of smile with which they were spoken completely overpowered Mr. Lester; but the doctor, who was still present, would not permit another word.

"You destroy his only chance," he

said ; and after that nothing would have induced Mr. Lester to let Cheriton speak to him. That evening, however, when he was alone with Alvar, Cherry's confused thoughts cleared themselves a little. He had been told to be hopeful, and he did not feel himself to be dying ! while with his whole heart he wished for life—the young bright life that was so full of love and joy, of which no outward trouble, no wearing anxiety, and no cold and selfish discontent had rendered him weary. Home and friends, the long lines of moorland that were shining in the sunset light, the hard work in the world behind and before him, the answering love of the woman whom he had chosen, were all beautiful and good to him; he felt no need of rest, no lack of joy.

He prayed for his life, not because he was afraid to die, but because he wished to live ; and when, with a sort of awful, solemn curiosity, he tried to realize that death might be his portion, his thoughts, not quite under his own control, turned

forcibly to those near to him. If he was
to die, there were things he must say to
his father, to Jack, to Alvar, a hundred
messages to his friends in the village—
they would let him see Mr. Ellesmere then
—when it did not matter how much he
hurt himself by speaking; but one thing
could not wait—

"Alvar, I *must* say something."

"Yes, I can hear," said Alvar, seeing
the necessity, and leaning towards him.

"When there is no chance, you will tell
me?"

"Yes."

"But I must tell you about—her—a
secret."

"I will keep it. Some one you love?"

"It is Ruth; we are engaged. Does
she know—this?"

Alvar's surprise was intense; but he
answered quietly,—

"I suppose that Virginia will have told
her."

"Let her know; it would be worse later.
Write to her—you—when it is hopeless."

" Yes," said Alvar.

"My love—my one love ! And say she must come and see me once more. She will—*I* would go anywhere."

" Hush, hush ! my brother; I understand you. I am to find out if Virginia has written to her cousin; and if you are worse, I write and ask her if she will come. I will do it."

" Thanks. I can't thank you. God knows how I love her."

" Not one more word," said Alvar, steadily. " Now you must rest."

" I shall get better," said Cherry.

But as the pain grew fiercer, and his strength grew less, this security failed; and then it was well indeed for Cheriton that, be his desires what they might, he believed with all his warm heart that it was a loving Hand that had given him life both here and hereafter.

Time passed on, and Cheriton still lay in great danger and suffering. It was a sorrowful Sunday in Oakby when his name headed the list of sick persons who were

prayed for in church. Every one could
tell of some boyish prank, some merry
saying, some act of kindness that he had
done; and now that he was believed to be
dying, be the facts what they might, there
was a sort of sense that he had been
deprived of his rights by his foreign
brother.

"It had a deal better a' been yon black-
bearded chap. What's he to us?" many
a one muttered.

Alas! that the thought would intrude
itself into the father's mind, spite of the
gratitude he could not but feel!

But Alvar went on with his anxious
watching, heeding no one but his brother.
That Sunday was a day of great suffering
and suspense, and all through the afternoon came lads from the outlying farms,
children from the village, messengers from
half the neighbourhood to hear the last
report. Silence and quiet were still so
forcibly insisted on, that even Mr. Lester
was advised by the doctor to keep out of
his son's room; but Mr. Ellesmere came

up to the house at his request and waited, for all thought that the useless prohibition would soon be taken away; and in the meantime his presence was a support to the father and grandmother, the latter of whom, at least, could bear to hear Cheriton praised.

Towards evening, Alvar, who had scarcely stirred all day, was sent downstairs by Mr. Adamson to get some food, and as he came into the dining-room, where the customary Sunday tea was laid on the table, he was greeted with a start of alarm. The two poor boys, tired, hungry, and frightened, had arrived but a few minutes before, and were standing about silent and awestruck.

Jack leant on the mantelpiece, with his lips shut as if they would never unclose again; Bob was staring out of the window; Nettie sat forlorn on one of a long row of chairs. Not one of them made an attempt to comfort or to speak to the others; they were almost as inaccessible in the sullen intensity of their grief as the two dogs, who, poor things! shared it, as they sat staring at Nettie, as dogs will when they do not comprehend the situation.

Alvar, with his olive face and grave dark eyes, looked, after all his fatigue, less changed than Jack, who was deadly pale, and hardly able to control his trembling.

"Ah! Jack," said Alvar, in his soft, slow tones, "he will be glad to hear that you are come!"

Jack did not speak at first, and Alvar, as silent as the rest, went up to the table an poured out some claret and took some bread.

"It's quite hopeless, I suppose?" said Jack, suddenly.

"No, do not say so!" said Alvar, half fiercely. "It is not so; but, oh, we fear it!" he added, in a voice of inexpressible melancholy.

Jack could not utter another word—he was half choking; but Nettie, unable to restrain herself any longer, began to cry piteously.

"Don't Nettie," said Bob, savagely.

"Ah!" said Alvar, "poor child, she is breaking her heart!" he went over to her, and took her in his arms and kissed her. "Poor little sister!" he said. "Ah! how we love him!"

The simple expression of the thought that was aching in the minds of all of them seemed to give a sort of relief. Nettie submitted to be caressed and soothed, and the boys came a little closer, and gave themselves the comfort of looking as wretched as they felt.

"Now I must eat some supper, for I dare not stay," said Alvar; "and you— you have been travelling—come and take some."

The poor boys began to find out how hungry they were, and Bob began to eat heartily; while the force of example made Jack take a few mouthfuls, till the vicar came into the room.

"Jack," he said quietly, "Cherry is so very anxious to see you that Mr. Adamson gives leave for you to go for one moment. Not the twins—they must wait a little. Can you stand it?"

" Yes, sir," said Jack, though, great strong fellow as he was, his knees trembled.

" Then, Alvar, are you ready? Have you really eaten and rested? You had better take him in."

Jack stood for a moment beside the bed, without attempting a word, hardly able to see that Cherry smiled at him, till he felt the hot fingers clasp his with more strength than he had looked for, and his hand was put into Alvar's, while Cheriton held them both, and whispered, " Jack, you *will*—"

" Yes, Cherry, I will," said Jack, understanding him. " I will, always."

" There, that must be enough," said Alvar. " Jack is very good—he shall come again."

" Oh! don't send me quite away," whispered Jack, as they moved a little. " Let me stay outside. I could go errands—I'll not stir."

Alvar nodded, and Jack went out into the deserted gallery, where, of course, he and Bob were not to sleep at present. The old sitting-room was full of things required

by the nurses, and Jack sat down on a
little window-seat in the passage, which
looked out towards the stables. He saw
Bob and Nettie arm-in-arm, trying to dis-
tract their minds by visiting their pets,
and his grandmother, too, coming slowly
and heavily to look at her poultry. He
had not seen his father, and dreaded the
thought of the meeting. Idly he watched
the ordinary movement of the servants, the
inquirers coming and going, and he thought
of the brother, best loved of all and most
loving—oh! if he could but hear Cherry
laugh at him again!

Upstairs all was silent, save for poor
Cheriton's painful cough and difficult
breathing; and presently it seemed to Jack
that the cough was less frequent, till, after
an interval of stillness, the doctor came
out. Jack's heart stood still. Was this
the fatal summons?

"Your brother is asleep," said Mr.
Adamson. "I feel more hopeful. I am
obliged to go, but I shall be here early.
Every one who is not wanted had better go
to bed."

He went downstairs as he spoke, but
Jack remained where he was, thinking he
might be at least useful in taking messages
or calling people. He had never sat up all
night before, and, anxious as he was, the
hours were wofully long.

Once or twice his grandmother came to
the head of the stairs, and Jack signalled
that all was quiet. At last, over the stable
clock, the dawn came creeping up; there
was the solitary note of a bird, then a
great twitter and the cawing of the rooks.

Jack put his head out of the window, and
felt the fresh, sharp air blowing in his face.
A cock crowed—would it wake Cherry?
Some one touched him on the shoulder;
he drew his head in, and Alvar stood by his
side.

" He is much better," he said. " He has
been so long asleep, and now the pain is less,
and he can breathe—he is much better."

Jack was afraid to speak, but he gave
Alvar's hand a great squeeze.

" Now, will you go and tell my father
this? Ah, how he will rejoice! But do
not let him come."

Jack sped downstairs and to his father's door, which opened at the sound of a foot-step.

"Papa, he is better. Alvar says he will get well."

Half a dozen hasty questions and an-swers, then Mr. Lester put Jack away from him and shut his door.

They could hardly believe that the relief was more than a respite, but the gleam of hope brightened as the day advanced. Cherry slept again, and woke, able to speak and say that he was better.

"And I must tell you, sir," said Mr. Adamson, afterwards, "that it is in a great measure owing to your son's good nur-sing."

Mr. Lester turned round to Alvar, who was beside him.

"I owe you a debt nothing can repay. I can never thank you for my boy's life," he said, warmly.

"Ah, do you *thank* me? You insult me!" cried Alvar, suddenly and fiercely. "Is he more to you than to me—my one

friend—my brother—*Cherito mio !*" And,
completely overcome, Alvar clasped his
hands over his face and dashed out of the
room.

Jack followed; but his admiration of
Alvar's self-control was somewhat shaken
by the sort of fury of indignation and emotion that seemed to stifle him, as he poured
out a torrent of words, half Spanish, half
English, walking about the room and shed-
ding tears of excitement.

" I say," said Jack, " they won't let *you*
go in to Cherry next, and then what will
he do ? "

Alvar subsided after a few moments, and
said, simply and rather sadly,—

" It is that my father does not understand me. But no matter—Cherry is
better—all is right now."

CHAPTER XX.

FACE TO FACE.

" And with such words—a lie !—a lie !
She broke my heart and flung it by."

IN the early days of August, after as long
a delay as she could find excuse for, Ruth
Seyton returned to Elderthwaite, knowing
that Rupert was to come next week to
Oakby for the grouse shooting, and that
Cheriton was ready to claim her promise;
for as she came on the very day of her
arrival to a garden-party at Mrs. Ellesmere's, she held in her pocket a letter
written in defiance of her prohibition, urg-
ing her to let him speak to her again, and
full of love and longing for her presence.

She knew that Rupert was coming, for
the quarrel between them was at an end.
Ruth had been very dull and desolate during

her quiet visit to some old friends of her
mother's, very much shocked at hearing
from Virginia of Cherry's illness, and more
self-reproachful for having let him linger
in the damp shrubberies by her side than
for the greater injury she had done him.

She wrote on the spur of the moment,
and sent Alvar a kind message of sympathy;
but every day her promise to Cheriton
seemed more unreal, and when at last
Rupert came, ashamed of the foolish dispute, and only wanting to laugh at and
forget it, she yielded to his first word, and,
though a little hurt to find how lightly he
could regard a lover's quarrel, was too
happy to forgive and be forgiven. But
one thing she knew that he would not
have forgiven, and that was her reception
of Cheriton's offer, and though it had
never entered into her theories of life to
deceive the real lover, she let it pass un-
confessed—nay, let Rupert suppose, though
she did not put it in words, that she had
discovered " Cheriton's folly " in time to
put it aside.

That she must shortly meet them both, and in each other's presence, was the one thought in her mind, even while she heard from Virginia that Cherry was almost well again, and detected a touch of chagrin in her eager account of Alvar's clever and constant care. " No, she had not seen him yesterday, but they would all meet to-day."

Still it was startling, when the two girls came out into the garden of the rectory, to see in the sunshine Cheriton Lester with a mallet in his hand, looking tall and delicate, but with a face of eager greeting turned full on her own.

In another moment he held her hand in a close, tight grasp, as she dropped her eyes and hoped that he was better.

" Quite well now," said Cheriton, in a tone that Ruth fancied every one must interpret truly.

" That is, when he obeys orders," said another voice; and Ruth felt her heart stand still, for Rupert came up to Cheriton's side and held out his hand to her.

For the first time in her life she was

sorry to see him. She could have screamed
with the surprise, and her face betrayed
an agitation that made Cheriton's heart
leap, as he attributed it to her meeting
with him after his dangerous illness.

"I am quite well," he repeated. "I
am not going to give any more trouble, I
hope, now."

Rupert looked unusually full of spirits.
"Good news," he whispered to Ruth, with
a smile of triumph. She could hardly
smile back at him. Alvar now came up
and spoke to them. He looked very grave;
as Ruth fancied, reproachful.

Some one asked Ruth to play croquet,
and she declined; then felt as if the game
would have been a refuge. But she took
what seemed the lesser risk, and walked
away with Rupert; and Cheriton tried in
vain for the opportunity of a word with
her—she eluded him, he hardly knew how.
The sense of suspicion and suspense which
had been growing all through the later
weeks of his recovery was coming to a
point.

Ruth seemed like a mocking fairy, like some unreliable vision, as he saw her smiling and gracious—nay, answered occasional remarks from her—but could never meet her eyes, nor obtain from her one real response.

These perpetual, impalpable rebuffs raised such a tumult in Cheriton's mind that he restrained himself with a forcible effort from some desperate measure which should oblige her to listen to him, while all his native reticence and pride could hardly afford him self-control enough to play his part without discovery.

An equal sense of baffled discomfort pressed on Virginia. She had very seldom seen a cloud on Alvar's brow; he never committed such an act of discourtesy as to be out of temper in her presence; but to-day he looked so stern as to prompt her to say, timidly, " Has anything vexed you, Alvar ? "

" How could I be vexed when you are here, queen of my heart ? " said Alvar, turning to her with a smile. " See, will

you come to get some strawberries—it is
hot ?"

"I would rather you told me when
things trouble you," said Virginia.

"It is not for you, *mi doña*, to hear of
things that are troubling," said Alvar, still
rather abstractedly.

"Are you still anxious about Cherry ?"
she persisted.

"*Ay de mi*, yes ; I am anxious about
him," said Alvar, sharply ; then changing,
"but I am ungallant to show you my
anxiety. That is not for you."

"Ah, how you misunderstand what I
want ! " she cried. "If I only knew what
you feel, if you would talk to me about
yourself ! But it is like giving an Eastern
lady fine dresses and sugar-plums."

The gentle Virginia was angry and
agitated. All through Cheriton's illness
she had felt herself kept at a distance by
Alvar, known herself unable to comfort
him, had suffered pangs that were like
enough to jealousy, to intensify themselves
by self-reproach. Yet she gloried in Alvar's

devotion to his brother, in his skill and
tenderness. Alvar did not perceive what
she wanted, and, moreover, was of course
unable to tell her the present cause of his
annoyance, at the existence of which he
did not wish her to guess.

" See now," he said, taking her hands
and kissing them, " how I am discourteous;
I am sulky, and I let you see it. Forgive
me, forgive me, it shall be so no more.
You shed tears; ah, my queen, they reproach me!"

Virginia yielded to his caresses and his
kindness, and blamed herself. Some day,
perhaps, in a quieter moment, she could
show him that she wanted to share his
troubles and not be protected from them.
In the meantime his presence was almost
enough.

Alvar, like some others of his name, was
a person of slow perceptions, and was apt
to be absorbed in one idea at a time. He
did not guess that while he paid Virginia
all the courtesy that he thought her due
she longed for a far closer union of spirits.

He was proud of being Cheriton's chief dependence during the tedious recovery that none of the others could bear to think incomplete, and to find that his tact and consideration made him a welcome companion when Jack's ponderous discussions were too great a fatigue. But he would not endure thanks, and after the outburst with which he had received his father's nobody proffered them. Not one of the others, full of anger with Ruth and of anxiety for Cheriton, could have abstained from fretting him with one word on the subject, as Alvar did all that afternoon and evening. But his mind was free to think of nothing else.

As for Ruth, the moment that should have been full of unalloyed bliss for her, the moment when Rupert told her that concealment was no longer necessary, was distracted ·by the terror of discovery.

Rupert had to tell her that the sale of a farm, effected on unusually advantageous terms, had made the declaration of his wishes possible to him, and he was now ready to present himself before her guardians and ask their consent to a regular engagement. Ruth was about to go back to her grandmother, and all might now be well. Ruth did not know how to be glad; she could not tell how deeply the Lesters might blame her. Her one hope was in Cheriton's generosity, and to him at least she must tell the whole truth.

" To-morrow I shall come and see you," he said gravely, as he wished her good-night, and she managed to give him an assenting glance, but he knew that she was treating him ill, and tormented himself with a thousand fancies—that his illness had changed him, that something during their separation had changed her. He said nothing, but the next day started alone for Elderthwaite.

It was a bright morning, with a clear blue sky. Cheriton passed into the wood and through the flickering shadows of the larches. He did not spend the time of his walk in forming any plans as to how he should meet Ruth; he set his mind on the one fact that a meeting was certain. But perhaps the brightness of the morning influenced his mood, for as he came out on to the bit of bare hill-side that divided the wood from the Elderthwaite property, a certain happiness of anticipation possessed him—circumstances might account for the discomfort of the preceding day, Ruth's eyes might once more meet his own, her voice once more tell him that she loved him.

The bit of fell was divided from Mr. Seyton's plantation [by a low stone wall, mossy, and overgrown with clumps of harebells and parsley fern, and half smothered by the tall brackens and brambles that grew on either side of it. Beyond were a few stunted, ill-grown oak-trees, with a wild undergrowth of hazel.

As Cheriton came across the soft, smooth turf of the hill-side, he became aware that some one was sitting on the wall beside the wide gap that led into the plantation, and he quickened his steps with a thrill of hope as he recognized Ruth. She stood up as he approached and waited for him, as he exclaimed eagerly,—

" This is too good of you ! "

" Oh, no ! " said Ruth, and began to cry.

Her eyes were red already, and with her curly hair less deftly arranged than usual, and her little black hat pushed back from her face, she had an air indescribably childish and forlorn.

Every thought of resentment passed from Cheriton's mind, he was by her side in a moment, entreating to be told of her trouble, and in his presence the telling of her story was so dreadful to her that perhaps nothing but the knowledge of Rupert's neighbourhood could have induced her to do it. Ruth hated to be in disgrace, and genuine as were her tears, she was not without a thought of prepossessing him in her favour. But she could not run the risk of Rupert's suddenly coming through the fir-wood.

" Please come this way," she said, breaking from him and skirting along inside the wall till they were out of sight of the pathway. Then she began, averting her face and plucking at the fern-leaves in the wall.

" I—I don't know how to tell you, but you are so good and kind and generous, so much—*much* better than I am—you won't be hard on me."

" It doesn't take much goodness to make me feel for your trouble," said Cheriton, tenderly. " Tell me, my love, and see if I am hard."

" Every one *is* hard on a girl who has been as foolish as I have."

Cheriton began to think that she was going to tell him of some undue encouragement given to some other lover in his absence or before her promise to him, and to believe that here was the explanation of all that had perplexed him.

" I shall never be offended when you tell me that I have no cause for offence," he said, putting his hand down on hers as she fingered the fern-leaves.

"*Indeed*, I would not have deceived you so long, but for your illness," said Ruth, a little more firmly.

"Deceived me! Dearest, don't use such hard words of yourself. Tell me what all this means. What fancy is this?"

"Will you promise—promise me to be generous and to forgive me? Oh, you may ruin all my life if you will," said Ruth, passionately.

"*I* ruin *your* life! ah, you little know! When my life was given back to me, I was glad because it belonged to you," said Cheriton, faltering in his earnestness.

"Then oh! Cherry, Cherry," cried Ruth, suddenly turning on him and clasping her hands, "then give me back my foolish promise—forget it altogether—let us be friends as we were when I was a little girl. Oh, Cherry, forgive me—I cannot—cannot do it!"

"What can you mean?" said Cheriton, slowly, and with so little evidence of surprise that Ruth took courage to go on.

"Cherry!" she repeated, as if clinging

to the name that marked her old relation to him; "Cherry, a long time ago—last spring, I was engaged to some one else—to your cousin; but it suited him—us—to say nothing of it at first. And oh! I was jealous and foolish, and we quarrelled, and I was in a passion, and thought to show him I didn't care. And you came that day at Milford, and I knew how good you were, and you begged so hard I couldn't resist you—you gave me no time. And then very soon he came back, and I knew I had made a mistake. I would have told you at once, indeed I would, but for your illness. How could I then?"

Cheriton stood looking at her, and while she spoke, his astonished gaze grew stern and piercing, till she shrank from him and turned away. Then he said, with a sort of incredulous amazement, with which rising anger contended,—

"Then you *never* meant what you said? When you told me that you loved me, it was false—you did not mean to give yourself to me? You kissed me to deceive me?"

" Oh, Cheriton ! " sobbed Ruth, covering her face, " don't—don't put it like that. I was very—very foolish—very wicked, but it was not all plain in that way. Won't you forgive me ? I was so very unhappy ! I thought you were always kind—"

" Kind ! " ejaculated Cheriton. " There is only one way of putting it ! Which is your lover, to which of us are you promised, to Rupert or to me ? "

Anger, scorn, and a pain as yet hardly felt, intensified Cheriton's accent. She had expected him to plead for himself, to bemoan his loss, and instead she shrank and quailed before his judgment of her deceit. His last words awoke a spark of defiance, and suddenly, desperately, she faced him and said, clearly,—

" To Rupert."

Cheriton put his hand back and leant against the wall. He was beginning to feel the force of the blow. After a moment he raised his head, and looked at her again, with a face now pale and mournful.

"Oh, Ruth, is it indeed so? Have I nothing to hope—nothing even to *remember?*" Did you *never* mean it—never?"

"I was so angry—so miserable that I was mad," faltered Ruth. "I thought *he* was false to *me.*"

"So you took me in to make up for it?" said Cheriton roughly, his indignation again gaining ground. "Well, I should thank you for at last undeceiving me!"

He turned as if to go; but Ruth sobbed out, "I know it was very wrong, indeed I am sorry for you. I can never, never be happy, if you don't forgive me."

"What can you mean by forgiving?" said Cheriton bitterly. "I wish I had died before I knew this! You have deceived me and made a fool of me, while I thought you—I thought you—"

"Then," cried Ruth, stung by the change of feeling his words implied, "you can tell them all about it if you will, and ruin me!"

"What!" exclaimed Cheriton, starting upright. "Is *that* what you can think

possible? Is *that* why you are crying?
You may be perfectly *happy!* The promise you had the prudence to exact has
been unbroken. No! when I thought that
I was dying, I told Alvar that *you* might
be spared any shock. Neither he nor I
are likely to speak of it further. I had
better wish you good-morning."

It was Cheriton whose love had been
scorned, whose hopes had all been dashed
to the ground in the last half-hour, and
who had received a blow that had changed
the world for him; but it had come in
such a form that the injured self-respect
struggled for self-preservation. The first
effect on his clear, upright nature was incredulous anger, a sense of resistance, of
shame and scorn, that, all-contending and
half-suppressed, made him terrible to Ruth,
whose self-deceit had expected quite another
reception of her words. She had shrunk
from the idea of giving him pain, had
dreaded the confession of her own mis-
deeds; but she had indemnified her conscience to herself for ill-treating Cheriton

by a sort of unnatural and unreal admiration of what she called his goodness; which seemed to her to render self-abnegation natural, if not easy, to him.

She, with her passionate feelings, her warm heart, might be forgiven for error; but he, since he was high-principled and religious, would surely make it easier for her, would stand in an ideal relation to her and tell her that "her happiness was dearer than his own." "Good" people were capable of that sort of self-sacrificing devotion. She thought, as many do, that Cheriton's battle was less hard to fight, because he had hitherto had the strength to win it. Poor boy, it had come to the forlorn hope now! He only knew that he must not turn and fly.

As Ruth looked up at him all tear-stained and deprecatory, his mood changed.

"Oh, Ruth, Ruth—Ruth!" he cried, as he turned away, "and I loved you so!"

But he left her without a touch of the hand; without a parting, without a pardon. No other relations could replace for him those she had destroyed. Ruth watched him hurry across the fell and into the fir-wood, and then, as she sank down among the ferns and gave way to a final burst of misery, she thought to herself, "Oh, Rupert, Rupert, what I have endured for your sake!"

CHAPTER XXI.

IN THE THICK OF THE FIGHT.

"Oh, that 'twere I had been false—not she !"

In the meantime the unconscious Rupert
was strolling up and down in front of the
house waiting for his uncle to come out,
and intending to take him into his confidence and ask for his good offices with
Ruth's guardians. It was well for her that
he had no suspicion of what was passing;
for little as she guessed it, he would have
greatly resented her treachery towards
Cheriton as well as towards himself. But
Rupert was in high spirits, and when Mr.
Lester joined him, he told his tale with
the best grace that he could. His uncle
was pleased with the news, and questioned
him pretty closely upon all its details,

shook his head over the previous difficulties which Rupert admitted, told him that he was quite right to be open with him, congratulated him when he owned to having met with success with the lady herself, and, pleased with being consulted, threw himself heart and soul into the matter.

As they came up towards the back of the house, they met Alvar, who, rather hastily, asked if they had seen Cheriton.

"He went to take a walk. I am afraid he will be tired," he explained.

"Eh, Alvar, you're too fidgety," said his father good-humouredly. "There's Cheriton, looking at the puppies."

Alvar looked, and beheld a group gathered in the doorway of a great barn, the figures standing out clear in the sunshine against the dark shadow behind. Nettie was standing in the centre with her arms apparently full of whining little puppies; the mother, a handsome retriever, was yelping and whining near. Buffer was barking and dancing in a state of frantic jealousy beside her. Bob and Jack were disputing over the merits of the puppies. Dick Seyton, with a cigar in his mouth, was leaning lazily against the barn door, while Cheriton, looking, to Alvar's anxious eyes, startlingly pale, was standing near.

"But say, Cherry, say," urged Nettie, "which of them are to be kept? Don't you think this is the best of all?"

"That," interrupted Bob, "that one will never be worth anything. Look, Cherry, this one's head—"

"Bob, what are you about here at this time in the morning?" said his father. "I told you I must have some work done these holidays. Be off with you at once."

"Cherry said yesterday he would come and help me," growled Bob.

"I want him," said Mr. Lester. "Got a piece of news for you, Cherry. No secret, Rupert, I suppose?"

"I'll tell Cherry presently," said Rupert, thinking the audience large and embarrassing.

Cheriton started, and the unseeing look

went out of his eyes, and for one moment he looked at Rupert as if he could have knocked him down. Then the reflection of his own look on Alvar's face brought back the instinct of concealment, the self-respect that held its own, while all their voices sounded strange and confused, and he could not tell how often his father had spoken to him or how long ago.

"I think I can guess your news," he said. "But I must go in. Come back to the house with me, Rupert."

He spoke rather slowly, but much in his usual manner. Rupert was aware that the news might not be altogether pleasant to him; but he had the tact to turn away with him at once; while Alvar watched them in utter surprise, the wildest surmises floating through his mind. But what Cherry wanted was to hear whether Rupert would confirm what Ruth had told him; somehow he could not feel sure if it were true.

"How long have you been engaged?" he said; "that was what you were going to tell me, wasn't it?"

"My uncle is frightfully indiscreet," said Rupert, with a conscious laugh. "Nothing has been settled yet with the authorities; but we have understood each other for some time. She—she's one in a thousand, and I don't deserve my luck."

Rupert was very nervous; he had always thought that Cheriton had a boyish fancy for Ruth, though he was far from imagining its extent, and he was divided between a sense of triumph over him and a most real desire not to let the triumph be apparent, or to give him unnecessary pain. Being successful, he could afford to be generous, and talked on fast lest Cherry should say something for which he might afterwards be sorry.

"I suppose we haven't kept our secret so well as we thought," he said, laughing, "as you guessed it so quickly. All last spring I was afraid of Alvar's observations."

"Did Alvar know? He might have— he might—?" Cheriton stopped abruptly,

conscious only of passion hitherto unknown.   He never marvelled afterwards at
tales of sudden wild revenge.   In that first
hour of bitter wrong he could have killed
Rupert, had a weapon been in his hand,
have challenged him to a deadly duel, had
such a thought been instinctive to his
generation.   Rupert did not look at him,
or the wrath in his eyes must have betrayed him.   He longed to revenge himself,
to tell Rupert all ; even his sense of honour
shook and faltered in the storm.   " She
promised *me !*   She kissed *me !* "   The
words seemed to sound in his ears, something within held them back from his lips.
Another moment, and Alvar touched his
arm.

" Come in, Cherito, the wind is cold," he
said.   " Come in with me."

Rupert, glad to close the interview, little
as he guessed how it might have ended,
turned away, saying, with a half-laugh, " I
must go and check Uncle Gerrald's com-
munications ; they are *too* premature."

Then Cheriton felt himself tremble from

head to foot; he knew that Alvar was talking, uttering words of vehement sympathy, but he could not tell what they were.

"You came in time—you came in time to save me!" said Cheriton wildly, as his senses began to recover their balance. He turned away his face for a few moments, then spoke collectedly.

"Thank you. That is all over now! You see I'm not strong yet. You will not see me like this again. The one thing is to prevent any one from guessing, above all my father."

"But, my brother, how can you—you cannot conceal from all that you suffer?" said Alvar, dismayed.

"Cannot I? I *will*," said Cheriton, with his mouth set, while his hands still trembled.

"Why? *You* have done no wrong," said Alvar. "Are you the first who has been deceived by a faithless woman? She is but a woman, my brother; there are others. You feel now that you could stab

your rival to revenge yourself. Ah, that
will pass; she's only a woman. Heavens!
I tore my hair. I wept. I told all my
friends of my despair; it was the sooner
over. You will find others."

"We usually keep our disappointments
to ourselves," said Cheriton coldly. "I
could not forgive any betrayal. Now I'll
go in by myself. I'll come down to lunch.
As you say, I'm not the first fellow who
has been made a fool of."

"What will he do?" thought Alvar as
he reluctantly left him. "He would forgive his rival sooner than himself. They
pretend to feel nothing, my brothers, that
gives them much trouble. If I were to
tell a falsehood to please them, they would
despise me; but Cherito will tell many
falsehoods to hide that he grieves."

Cheriton gathered himself up enough to
hide his rage and grief, hardly enough in
any way to struggle with them, and the
suffering was as uncontrollable and as
exhausting as the pain and fever of his
late illness. It shut out even more com-

pletely the remembrance of anything but
his own sensations. And it was all so
bitter—he felt the injury so keenly—he had
not yet power to feel the loss. He kept
up well, however, and during the next two
or three days his father saw nothing amiss;
while Alvar, though anxious about his
health, regarded the misery as a phase
that must have its way. But Nettie
declared that Cherry was cross, and Jack,
who had lately acquired the habit of
noticing him, felt that he was not himself.
It was difficult to define; but it seemed to
him as if his brother never looked, spoke
or acted exactly as might have been
expected. Things seemed to pass him
by.

The twelfth of August proving hopelessly wet and wild, even Mr. Lester could
not think his joining the shooting party
allowable, and Cheriton expressed a
proper amount of disappointment; but
Jack recollected that when they had all
been speculating on the weather the night
before, Cherry had hardly turned his head

to look at it. He would not let Alvar stay
at home with him, and felt glad to be free
from observation.

In the meantime matters had not gone
much more pleasantly at Elderthwaite.
Ruth was in such dread of discovery that
even in Rupert's presence she could not be
at ease. Her conscience reproached her,
and she was by no means sure that
Rupert was quite unsuspicious, for he
talked a good deal about his cousin, and
once said that he thought him much
changed by his illness. Neither was she
happy with Virginia, towards whom a certain amount of confidence was necessary,
as she could not lead her to suppose that
all had been freshly settled with Rupert;
and Virginia, who was usually reticent
and shy, questioned her closely as to
Rupert's behaviour and modes of action.
Indeed she marvelled at her cousin's
ignorance, for Alvar seemed to her to imply
displeasure in every look. He came seldom
to Elderthwaite, and, when there, scarcely
spoke of Cherry. Ruth could only hurry

her return to her grandmother, which was
to take place in a few days ; but an Oakby
dinner-party, in honour of the engagement, could not be avoided. Ruth dared
not have a head-ache or a cold, and in a
tremor most unlike her usual self she prepared to meet her two lovers face to face.
If Cheriton had any mercy for her, or any
feeling for himself, he would avoid her.
How little she had once thought ever to be
afraid of Cherry! But he was there, with
a flower in his coat, and plenty of conversation, apparently on very good terms
with Rupert, and facing the greeting with
entire composure. He even ate his dinner ;
he sat, not opposite Ruth, but low down
on the other side of the table, while she
had Alvar for her neighbour—a very silent
one, as Virginia, on his other side,
remarked with a sigh. It would have
been natural for her to talk to Rupert,
who sat on the other side of her, but she
felt Cheriton's eyes on her in all their
peculiar intenseness of expression. Ruth
was very sensitive, and they seemed to

mesmerize her; she grew absolutely pale, and she knew that Rupert saw it. How could Cheriton be so cruel!

Her white face and drooping lip flashed the same thought to Cheriton himself. What a coward he was thus to revenge himself! He turned his head away with a sudden rush of softening feeling. Disappointed love and jealousy had, she told him, driven her mad—what were they making of him? At least it was more manly to let her alone.

"Cheriton, I want a word with you," said Rupert, turning into the smoking-room when the party was over. "Of course, you have a right to refuse to answer me, but—I can't but observe your manner. Do you consider yourself in any way aggrieved by my engagement?"

It did not occur to Cheriton that, if Rupert had had full trust in Ruth, he would never have put such a question. He was conscious of such unusual feelings that he knew not how far he stood self-betrayed in manner. Rupert was his cousin, almost as intimate as a brother, and he could not resent the question quite as if it had come from a stranger. It could have been answered by a short negative, leaving the sting that had prompted it where it had been before. Full of passion and resentment as Cheriton still was, he could not *now* have broken his word and deliberately betrayed the girl who had betrayed him.

He was silent for a minute; still another part was open. At last he looked up at Rupert and said,—

"I made her an offer—she has refused me. Don't mind my way—there's an end of it."

"Cherry, you're a good fellow, a real good fellow—thank you!" said Rupert warmly. "I'm sorry, with all my heart."

"Don't think about me," repeated Cheriton rather stiffly. "But I'll say good-night."

He was so obviously putting a great force on himself that Rupert, feeling that he could not be the one to offer sympathy,

would not detain him; but as he gave
his hand a hearty squeeze, Cherry, with
another great effort, said,—

" I *do* wish her—happiness," then turned
away and hurried upstairs.

CHAPTER XXII.

STRUGGLING.

" And my faith is torn to a thousand scraps,
  And my heart feels ice while my words breathe flame."

IT was a wild, wet morning, some days
after the Oakby dinner-party. Summer
weather was apt in those regions to be in-
vaded in August by something very like
autumn; bits of brown and yellow appeared here and there among the green,
and fires became essential. To-day the
mist was driving past the windows of the
boys' sitting-room, blotting out the view,
till the wind rent it apart and showed dim
sweeps of distant moor.

Bob Lester was sitting at the table,
with his eyes fixed, *not* on the exceedingly
inky copy of Virgil before him, but on the
window, as he remarked dolefully,—

"Birds are wild enough already, without all this wind to make them worse."

Jack was writing at the other end of the table; Nettie, with an old waterproof cloak on, was kneeling on the window-seat, watching the weather, with Buffer, apparently similarly occupied, by her side; and Cheriton, with considerable sharpness of manner, was endeavouring to drive the Latin lesson into Bob's head.

For Bob was under discipline. Such a bad report of him had come from school as to idleness, troublesomeness, and general misbehaviour, that his father, after a private interview, the nature of which Bob did not disclose, had ordered a certain amount of work to be done every day, to be taken back to school, and had forbidden a gun or a fishing-rod to be touched till this was accomplished. Cherry in the early days of his convalescence, had received Bob's growls on the subject, and had offered to help him, as Jack's efforts as a tutor were not found to answer, and had actually coaxed a certain amount of

information into him. Lately, however,
the lessons had not gone off so well.
Cheriton had made a great point of them,
and held Bob as if in a vice by the force
of his will; but he was sarcastic instead
of playful, and contemptuous instead of
encouraging, and now lost patience, laying
down his book and speaking in a cutting,
incisive tone that made Bob start. and
stare.

" We have all got aims in life, I suppose;
I wish we were all as likely to succeed in
them as you are, Bob."

" I haven't got an aim in life," said Bob,
turning round as if affronted.

" No ? I thought your aim was to be
the greatest dunce in the county. It's
well to know one's own line, and do a thing
well while one's about it. A low aim's a
mistake in all things."

Jack laid down his pen, and stared hard
at Cheriton. Bob waited unconscious,
expecting the smile and twinkle that took
the sting out of all Cherry's mischief, but
none came.

" Come now, you needn't be down on a fellow in that way," he said, angrily. " My line mayn't be yours, but I'll—I'll stick to it one day."

" I just observed that you were sticking to it now, heart and soul. Let all your wits lie fallow; with the skill and energy you are showing at present, you may get to the level of a ploughboy in time."

" I say, Cherry," said Jack, " that's a little strong."

Bob shut the book with a bang and stood up.

" I'm not going to stand that," he said ; and Cheriton recollected himself and coloured. " I beg your pardon, Bob," he said. " It was too bad. I—I was only joking. Will you go on now ? "

" No," said Bob. " I won't be made game of."

" You tire Cherry to death," said Jack. " No wonder he loses patience."

" *I* didn't ask him to do it," said Bob. " Nettie, where are you going? "

" Out," said Nettie, briefly.

"Then I'm going too," said Bob, following her; while Cheriton wearily threw himself down on the cushions in the window-seat and in his turn stared out at the mist. Jack sat and watched him. He had never uttered a word even to Alvar, but he was full of anxiety. What was the matter with Cherry?

He was lively enough at meal-times and with his father and grandmother; he had resumed all his usual habits, except that the bad weather had prevented him from going out shooting. He had laughed at Alvar for being over-anxious about him, and had taken a great deal of unnecessary trouble about sundry village matters and affairs at home. He had talked what Alvar called "philosophy" to Jack with unusual seriousness; and yet Jack, with whom perhaps he was least on his guard, missed something. And then Mrs. Ellesmere had remarked that she did not like to see Cheriton with such a pink colour and such black circles round his eyes, and had warned her husband not to let him fatigue himself on some walk they were taking. Surely Cherry coughed oftener, and was more easily tired, than he had been ten days ago.

Jack could bear it no longer, and began, severely—

" Cherry, you shouldn't worry yourself with Bob. It's too much for you."

" Not generally," said Cheriton. " I'm tired to-day."

" What's the matter with you, Cherry ? " said Jack, coming nearer.

" The matter ? " said Cherry, sitting up, and laughing more in his usual way. " What should be the matter ? Are you taking a leaf out of Alvar's book ? Of course, one isn't very strong after such an illness, and I don't sleep always. I shall go away, I think, soon, and then I shall be right enough."

" Where will you go to ? Let me go with you. Or must it be Alvar ? "

" Oh, I shall be best alone. Don't worry, Jack. I'm no worse, really."

Poor Cheriton ! His efforts at con-

cealment, made half in pride, and half
in consideration, were not very successful.

As he lay awake through the long
nights, Ruth's woeful look and appealing
eyes haunted him, and as he remembered
their parting, his own bitter scorn came
back on him with a pang, partly, no doubt,
because she was still irresistible to him,
but partly, also, because he knew that *he*
had felt the temptation under which *she*
had fallen. She had treated him shame-
fully; and she declared that her excuse
was, if excuse it could be called, that she
had been driven so frantic by her mis-
judgment of Rupert, that anything seemed
legitimate that would give him pain. She
had transgressed every code of womanly
honour, and had cost Cheriton pain beyond
expression by obeying a sudden impulse of
mortified passion. Any sort of revenge on
her by Cheriton was at least as incom-
patible with any standard of social obligation, no extra high principle was needed
to condemn it; to take such a blow and

be silent over it seemed a mere matter of course. Cheriton was very high-prin-cipled, he had conquered in his time strong temptations; moreover, he was more than commonly loving and tender, and yet he felt that there had been more than one moment when he might have committed this utter baseness. He forgot for a moment that he *had* conquered, that strength, however unconscious, had come to him from his former struggles, and had held him back; he felt that if this were possible to him, he was safe from nothing. He shuddered as he thought of his inter-view with Rupert, and his first prayer since the blow turned into a thanks-giving.

But any thought of his own conduct was soon swept away by the rush of regret and pain. She *had* failed him, however unworthy he might be to judge her; and as he remembered the many sweet and en-chanting moments that had led up to his final disappointment, he could not but feel that she had deliberately deceived him.

And yet—and yet—as he recalled her face
at the dinner-table, he knew that he would
have come back to her at a word; he felt
as if life was worth nothing without
her, as if father and brothers, home, interests, and ambitions had all lost their
charm. Cheriton retained enough com-
mand over himself to resolve to make head
against this state of mingled regret and
bitterness; he could not yet bring himself to accept it with any sort of submis-
sion; his feelings of gratitude and joy at
his returning strength seemed almost as
if they had been sent in mockery to
make disappointment more cruel. But
this thought brought its own remedy.
His life had been given back to him, not
surely only that he might endure this
fierce trial—something would come out of
the furnace. And when he remembered
what his well-being was to his father, the
resolution of self-conquest was made in
something else than pride. " God help
me. I'll learn my lesson!" he thought;
and he dimly felt that that lesson meant

more than putting a bold face on things,
or even than a surface recovery of spirits,
of the probability of which last he was of
course then no judge. It meant whether
this bitter trial was to leave him more or
less of a man than it found him—more of
a Christian if he would not be less of a
man.

It must not be supposed that Cheriton
at this time attained with any permanence
to such convictions—he worked his way
to them at intervals; but, after all, most
of his sleepless hours were spent in a hopeless involuntary recall of his past happiness. Ruth haunted him as if she had
been a spirit, and of course the over-
fatigue produced by the effort to force his
mind into its usual channels affected his
health, and made him still less able to
fight against his troubles.

He was very reluctant to confess himself beaten, and began to talk to Jack with
would-be eagerness about going to London
and beginning his reading for the bar. His
name had been entered at the Temple,

most of his " dinners " were eaten, and he
had never intended his time of waiting for
a brief to be an idle one. Presently his
father called him, and he started up and
went downstairs, while Jack went back to
his writing with divided attention, and dim
suspicions of the truth gaining ground.

Meanwhile Cheriton found himself called
to a conference in the study.

All the arrangements for Alvar's marriage had been deferred through Cheriton's
illness, and Mr. Lester felt it somewhat
strange that he should be the first person
who saw the need of recommencing them.
He told Alvar that he wished to speak to
him, and made a sort of apology to him
for Cheriton's presence by saying that he
wished him to hear the money arrangements
which he thought fit to make.

" I am sure, Alvar," said Mr. Lester, for-
mally, " you have shown great unselfishness
in putting your own affairs so completely
on one side during your brother's illness;
but now there is no longer any reason for
deferring the consideration of your mar-

riage, and I should be glad to know what plans you may have formed for the future."

" It is your wish, sir, that I should be married—soon ? " said Alvar, coolly and deferentially.

" Why—October was mentioned from the first, wasn't it ? " said Mr. Lester, with a sort of taken-aback manner that made Cheriton smile.

" Yes," said Alvar. " If that is your desire, and Mr. Seyton approves, I·should wish it."

" Why—why—haven't you settled it all with Virginia ? "

" I did not think one should trouble a lady with those matters, nor did I wish to marry while my brother might need me."

" That was very good of you ; but I hope by that time to be in London," said Cherry, decidedly, and with a look, conveying caution.

Alvar was silent for a moment, and then said, with what Cheriton called his princely air,—

"I shall then marry in October, and I will take my wife to visit my friends and my—other country."

"Why, yes; that would be very proper, no doubt; and I think you once told me that you wished to take a house in London."

"That would be good luck for me," said Cherry, by way of encouragement.

"Yes," said Alvar, "I wish it to be so."

Mr. Lester then entered into an explanation of the means which he was prepared to place at Alvar's disposal, talked of house rent and of Virginia's fortune, and said a few words on the amount of his own means, and what he meant to do for the younger ones. Nettie was provided for by her mother's fortune, a smaller proportion of which would be inherited by the sons also at their father's death. "But," as Mr. Lester concluded, "of course they all know that in the main they must look to their own exertions."

"Of course," said Cheriton.

Alvar looked very much surprised.

"The boys," he said, "yes; but I thought, my father, you would wish that Cheriton should be rich."

"Alvar," said Mr. Lester, rising and speaking with real dignity, "you misunderstand me. In such matters I can make no distinctions between my sons. Cheriton and his brothers stand exactly on the same footing. As for you, you will have to represent the old name, and keep the old place on its proper level. I shall not stint you of the means of doing so with ease and dignity."

Alvar cast down his eyes, and a curious look as of a sort of oppression passed over his face.

"That will be an obligation to me," he said, gravely. "You are most—honourable to me, my father."

"Not at all," said Mr. Lester. "I should not think of acting otherwise. Well —now you had better be off to Elderthwaite and settle all your affairs."

Alvar left the room, and Mr. Lester burst out,—

" I declare, there's something about that fellow that makes me feel as if I were a schoolboy!" Then, a little ashamed of the admission, he went on, " I like to see more ardour in a lad when his marriage is in question. Why, Rupert lived at Elderthwaite, while he was here!"

" We must make allowance for the difference of manners," said Cherry. " Alvar is very good to me. But, father, I don't think I shall be strong enough to shoot this month; it would be foolish to catch another cold; so I thought I should like a little trip somewhere soon—just a change before I settle down to work again."

" Why, yes," said Mr. Lester; " of course, if you wish, though we haven't had much good of you since you came home, my boy. Where do you want to go?"

" I don't know—to Paris, perhaps," said Cherry, on the spur of the moment. " Huntingford and Donaldson both asked me to join them this summer; so I shouldn't interfere with Alvar. Then, afterwards I can make all my arrangements for London."

"Well, yes," said Mr. Lester, reluctantly; "if you can't shoot, there's no use, of course, in your going to Milford or Ashrigg."

"Jack can go; it's time he went about a little, and he will be a better shot than I am soon. And when I come back, I'll be ready for anything."

Cherry's energy was quite natural enough to deceive his father, especially as he kept out of sight during this interview; but when he went away from the study, his heart suddenly failed him, and he felt as if he never should have the courage to set about carrying out the plans on which he had just been insisting.

CHAPTER XXIII.

MISGIVINGS.

"I looked for that which is not, nor can be."

A FEW days before Alvar's interview with his father, Rupert had left Oakby to make his personal application to Ruth Seyton's guardians, backed up by a letter from Mr. Lester, and by her own communication to her grandmother. Of course, nothing could be said of the six months of mutual understanding, and this concealment weighed lightly enough on Ruth's conscience. She vexed Virginia by her reserve on all the details of her engagement, but what really troubled her was her parting interview with Rupert, as they were alone together in the garden at Elderthwaite.

This had once been laid out in the Italian

style, with fountains, statues, and vases, stiff, neat paths, and little beds cut in the smooth turf and full of gay colour. Of all kinds of gardening, this kind can least bear neglect, and at Elderthwaite a few occasional turns with the scythe and a sprinkling of weedy-looking flowers did not suffice to make it a pleasant resort.

Ruth sat on the pedestal of a broken nymph by the side of a dried-up fountain. This garden was supposed to be "kept up," so some flaring yellow nasturtiums and other inexpensive flowers filled the little beds round. It was a dull day, and the weather was chilly, and Ruth in her crimson shawl looked by far the most cheerful object in the garden. Rupert had stuck some of the nasturtiums in her hat, and they suited her dark hair and warm, clear skin. After a great deal of talk, entirely satisfactory to both, Rupert said, lightly,—

"By the way, I thought I would take Master Cherry to task for his manner to you the other night."

"Cherry—his manner—what do you mean?" stammered Ruth, with changing colour.

"Well, I was rather sorry I had said anything about it, but he was very frank, poor boy, and told me you had refused him."

"I—I did not think you would have asked him such a question," said Ruth, hardly knowing what she said in the agony of fear, relief, and shame.

"Oh, well, we're almost like brothers, you know, and I was not going to have him make such great eyes at you for nothing. What had he to reproach you with?"

The words were more an exclamation than a question, but they terrified Ruth, and she pressed coaxingly up to Rupert, and said with a good deal of agitation,—

"Oh, I am very sorry—very; but—but of course I couldn't tell of him—could I? And he is so impetuous and so set on his own way! But I don't want you to be angry with him, poor boy, or—or with me, for, oh! my darling, we mustn't quarrel again, or it would kill me!"

" Is she afraid I shall find out how much encouragement she gave him ?" said Rupert in his teasing way.

" Oh! he didn't want much *encouragement*," said Ruth. " But there, never mind, he'll soon forget all about me. Did you think no one ever liked me but you ?"

Rupert's rejoinder was cut short by the appearance of Virginia, and Ruth ran towards her, for once glad to leave Rupert. She tried to persuade herself that she had told him no direct falsehood, but the memory of her two interviews with Cheriton lay heavy on her soul.

She knew that she had sinned against her own article of faith, her love for Rupert; and her perfect pride and glory in its perfection was marred. She had fallen below her own standard; she could no longer feel that she acted out her own ideal. Ruth was a girl capable of an ideal, though she had not set up a lofty one. Perhaps every one has some standard, however poor, and the crucial test of character may be whether we pull it down to suit our failures, or no. Ruth at this time was earnestly endeavouring to do so, but it did not come easy to her, and by way of set-off she occupied herself with being exceedingly kind to Virginia, whom she was beginning to consider injured, and in whom she recognized an unexpected warmth of resentment. Not that Virginia ever uttered a complaint of Alvar, but she avoided his name in so marked a manner, and looked so unhappy, that she was self-betrayed.

They were sitting together in the drawing-room on the day of Alvar's interview with Mr. Lester. It was a dreary, un-homelike-looking room on that wet, cloudy day, but Ruth, spite of misgivings, had a bright prosperous air as she sat writing to Rupert, curls, ribbons, and ornaments all in order, the deep red bands on her summer dress giving it a cheerful air even on a wet day.

Virginia was sitting in the window doing nothing; she was pale, and her white

dress with its elaborate flouncings had
seen more than one wearing. She did not
look expectant of a lover. Ruth watched
her for a little while, and then said,
slyly,—

> " He cometh not, she said,
> She said I am aweary, aweary ;
> I would that I were dead !"

" Ruth ! how can you ? " exclaimed
Virginia, indignantly. " Who would ex-
pect anybody on such a wet day as this ?
Of course I don't ? "

" Queenie ! " said Ruth, springing up
and kneeling down beside her, " I don't
like to see you look so miserable. If Don
Alvar is a lukewarm lover, he's not good
enough for my Queenie, and he shan't have
her. There ! "

" You have no right to say such a
thing, Ruth. I may be silly and foolish,
but I won't hear any one find fault with
him, not even you ! "

" Bravo, Queenie ! but I wasn't going
to find fault with him exactly. I daresay
he thinks it is all right enough, only—only
that's not *my* idea of a lover ! Give him

a little pull up, Queenie; scold him—if you can."

Virginia coloured, trembled, and scarcely refrained from tears.

" You make me reproach myself, Ruth," she said, " for being so silly and exacting. It ought to please me that Alvar is so good and kind, and that at last his people have found him out. It *does*—"

" Look ! " exclaimed Ruth, pointing out of window. " Who comes there? And your gown is crumpled, and your necktie is faded, and you're not fit to be seen ! Run—run and adorn yourself ! "

But Virginia hardly heard her, she was too eager to see Alvar for any delay, and, hurrying to the garden-door, she opened it, while Ruth recollected the awkward-ness of an interview with Alvar and fled. But he was far too punctilious to come into the drawing-room with his wet coat, hat, and umbrella, and he waved his hand to Virginia and went round to the front door, where, in the hall, he met Ruth, and acknowledged her as he passed with a stately bow that nearly annihilated her.

Virginia had meant to be distant and reproachful, but her resolutions always melted in Alvar's presence; he was so delightful to her that she forgot all her previous vexations. Demonstrative she never could be to him, but she contrived to say,—

"It *is* a long time since you were here, dear Alvar."

"Ah, yes," he said, " *mi doña,* too long indeed; but we have had people in the house, and Cherry is not strong enough to entertain them."

"How is he?" asked Virginia, feeling, as she always did, as if rebuked for selfishness.

"Pretty well; this rain is bad for him; he may not go out," said Alvar, who did not wish to represent Cheriton as specially unwell just then. "But see, *mi querida,* I have been talking to my father, and he gives me courage to speak of the future."

And then in the most deferential manner

Alvar unfolded his plans, ending by saying,—

"And will you come with me to Seville
that I may show my English bride to my
countrymen, and teach them what flowers
grow in England?"

"I would rather go to Spain than *anywhere* else," said Virginia, all misgivings
gone. "I hope they will—like me."

"Ah," said Alvar, smiling, "there is
no fear. They would not like those boys
—but you—they would worship!"

Virginia laughed gaily, and he continued
presently, touching the bow on her dress,—

"But this ribbon—it is not a pretty
colour. I am rude, but I do not like it."

"Oh, Alvar, I am very sorry. Ruth
said I ought to change it. I thought you
would not come, and I didn't care for my
ribbons. I *do* not care—except when you
see me."

There was a break in her voice as she
looked at Alvar with eyes full of pathetic
appeal for a response to the love she gave
him.

Alvar smiled tenderly.

" We will soon change it," he said, and, opening the glass door again, he picked two crimson roses that climbed over it, shook the rain-drops carefully from their petals, and then fastened them into Virginia's hair and dress. " There ! " he said, " that is the royal colour, the colour for my queen. See, I must have a share of it. Give me the rosebud."

Virginia stood for a moment with her eyes cast down. She could have thrown herself into Alvar's arms, and poured forth her feelings with a fervour of expression that might have startled him, but the doubt and timidity which she had never lost towards him restrained her ; she put the rose into his coat and was happy. The sun came out through the clouds, they strolled through the garden together, and Alvar talked to her about Spain, his stately old grandfather, his many cousins, and all the surroundings of his old life.

When he left her at length, and she ran indoors to Ruth, she was another creature

from the pale, lifeless girl who had watched
the rain-clouds in the morning.

Alvar, too, went home well pleased with
his morning, and ready to make himself
agreeable, and as he came through the
larch wood into the park, he suddenly en-
countered the twins.

Nettie was standing with her back to a
tree, a very shabby-looking book under
her arm. She was scarlet, and almost
sobbing with indignation. Bob was opposite to her, evidently having got the upper
hand in their dispute. He was talking in
a downright decisive voice, and ended
with,—

"And so I tell you, I won't have it."

"I don't care."

"If you do it again, I'll tell Cherry."

"Well, tell him, then! I'll tell him myself. *He* would do just the same, I know
he would."

"Then why do you get up in the morning and go out— ?"

Here Bob caught sight of Alvar and
stopped short.

" What is the matter with you two?
Why do you dispute?" said Alvar, good-
naturedly.

" Nothing," said Bob, shortly; "I was
only talking to Nettie."

" We were only talking," said Nettie;
and they walked away together, with a
manifest determination to exclude Alvar
from a share even in their quarrels. Interfering between the twins, Cheriton had
once said, was like interfering between
husband and wife; the peacemaker got the
worst of it.

Apparently Cheriton was experiencing
this truth, for when Alvar came in, he
heard sounds of lively discussion in the
library. His father was speaking in a loud,
clear voice, and with his Westmoreland
tones strongly marked, a sure sign that he
was in a passion. Jack was standing very
upright, looking impatient and important.
Cherry sat listening, but with an irritated
movement of the fingers, and a flush of
annoyance on his face. It had been a
rough time lately at Oakby, and Mr. Lester

was just anxious enough about Cheriton to be ready to find fault with him.

" No, Cheriton," he was saying, as Alvar entered, " I'll not hear a word of the kind. It's a fine result of your influence over the lads if it's to lead to this sort of mischief. Warn them ! I forbid it positively. You have made too much of these boys, letting them write to you at Oxford. Much good their writing does them, and lending them books beyond them. No, I'll do my duty by my tenants in every way—education and all; but there's a limit."

" But, father," said Cherry, " I can't make it out. Of course, if Wilson has seen the young Flemings in the copses, I'm very sorry ; but anyhow, it would be better to try to talk to them."

" No, I'll not have it done. Wilson has orders to watch to-night, and if they're caught, over to Hazelby they shall go, and no begging off for them."

" Oh, father," said Cherry, starting up ; " do let me go and see them this afternoon. I haven't been near them since I

was ill, and I'm sure I can find out the
truth of it.   It's ruin to a lad to get into a
row with the keepers, and they are capital
fellows.   Just let me try."

"What is the matter?" asked Alvar.

"Why," said his father, "some young
fellows that Cheriton has a special fancy
for, have been poaching in my copses!"

"Why, they deserve hanging for it!"
said Alvar.

"Hanging!" cried Jack.   "The evils
of the Game Laws—"

"Oh, nonsense, Jack.   Put that in your
'Essay on the Evils of all Sorts of Govern-
ments,'" said Cherry; then turning to the
squire, "But they are not poachers,
father."

"I will not be interfered with.   You
take too much on yourself," said Mr.
Lester; then, seeing Cheriton look first
blankly amazed, then angry, and finally
hurt beyond measure, he suddenly softened.

"Well, you can go and see them if you
wish.   Don't vex yourself, my lad; you

make too much of it. But you're looking
better than you did yesterday."

"Oh, my head ached yesterday," said
Cherry brightly ; but he looked up at his
father with a sudden pang and sense of in-
gratitude. Why could he care so little for
anything, so little for the Flemings, even
while he argued in their behalf? He lin-
gered a little, talking to his father, while
Jack returned to his essay "On the Evils
Inherent in every Existing Form of Government;" and then set off on his walk to the
Flemings' farm. He ought to care for
lads to whom he had taught their cricket
and their catechism, and who were much
of an age with himself and his brothers,
and often thought to resemble them,
being equally big, fair, and strong. He
talked and sympathized till the story of
certain wrongs was confided to him by
the younger one—how a certain "she"
had nearly driven him to bad courses,
but "she warn't worth going to the
bad for."

Cherry looked at the lad's serene and

ruddy face, and felt as if he might get a lesson.

Did all his culture and his principle and refinement only sap his powers of endurance?

"You're a brave fellow, Willie," he said, putting out his hand. "I wish—well, don't let me hear of your getting into trouble, or going with those poaching fellows."

"No, sir, not for her, nor for any lass. But—there's the old parson."

Cherry got up from the wall of the field where he had been sitting, and went to meet him.

"Ha, Cherry, my lad, glad to see you out again," said Parson Seyton, coming cheerily over the furrows. "Good-day t'ye, Willie; turnips look well."

Young Fleming touched his hat, and after a word or two, Cheriton asked Mr. Seyton if he were going Oakby way, as they might walk together; and, with a farewell to Fleming, they started down the hill.

"If I hadn't found you here, I should have been inclined to poach on Ellesmere's manor, and give young Willie a word of advice," said Mr. Seyton.

"I know. He has been getting in with the Ryders and Fowlers, and my father heard an exaggerated story about him and Ned being seen in our copses at night. I think that the Flemings are above taking to poaching; but Willie has been in a bad way."

"Hope your father'll catch some of my fellows; do 'em good," said the parson. "If he caught my nephew Dick, and shut him up for a bit, the place might be all the better. Hangs about all day, just like his father. He's after something, and I can't make out what."

"Sometimes I see him about with Bob."

"With Bob? Ha! you look about you, Cherry," said the parson, mysteriously. "My eyes are sharp. I knew when Miss Ruth and Captain Rupert had their little meetings; but then, I knew better than spoil sport."

"You knew more than most," said Cherry.

"Ay, and look here, Cherry," said the parson, stopping and looking full at him. "There's another thing I can see, and that is, when a man's in earnest and when he isn't; and when all's smooth and sweet to a girl, and when she looks this way and that for something that's wanting."

"I have nothing to do with my cousin's engagement," said Cherry, bewildered.

"Nay—nay, it's not your cousin. I don't believe in foreigners, Cherry; and Master Alvar isn't what I call a lover for a pretty girl that worships the ground he treads on. If he wants her money, why, a gentleman should keep up appearances at least."

Cheriton looked very much affronted.

"I don't know if you are aware," he said, "that my brother's marriage has just been fixed to take place in October; he was at Elderthwaite to-day. And for the rest, Alvar is very unselfish, and I have taken up a great deal of his time."

The parson looked at him with an odd sort of twinkle. " Ay, ay; I know all about that," he said; " but we old fellows know what we're about. Well, I turn off here; so good day to you, and mind my words."

Cheriton walked on, somewhat ruffled and disturbed. He knew the old parson would not have spoken as he had without some reason; and it crossed his mind that Bob must be engaged in some undesirable amusements with Dick; but if so,. what could he do? It was instinctive with Cheriton to try to do something when any difficulty was brought before him. Unselfish, loving, and, like all influential people, fond of influence, he had surrounded himself by calls on his energies and his interest. And now these surroundings were all unchanged, while he was changed utterly. The relations of son, brother, neighbour, friend, which he had filled so thoroughly, remained; and the feelings due to each seemed to have all died away, killed by the blow that had come upon him. He had never lived to himself, nor realized his life apart from the other lives in which it was bound up, or from his school, his college, and, most of all, his home; and now, with this great loss and pain, he suddenly found that he had a self behind it all—a self, fearfully strong, utterly absorbing; all the proportions of life were changed to him. Nothing seemed to matter but the chance of rest and relief. The plans he made had no heart in them; he felt as if the labour necessary for success in life was impossible, the success itself indifferent. His tastes were pure; the many temptations of life had been fairly met and conquered by him; but each one now seemed to look him in the face from a new point of view, and with new force. Soul as well as heart is risked in such an injury as Ruth had done him, and the more finely balanced perhaps the more easily overthrown. He did not cease to resist; but it was chiefly against the increasing weakness and languor which were sure in the end to prove irresistible to him.

CHAPTER XXIV.

A CRISIS.

" I will take a year out of my life and story."

ONE chilly morning, a week or so after these events, Virginia was sitting in the drawing-room, with a heap of patterns in her lap. She was choosing her wedding gown, and as she laid the glistening bits of silk and satin on the table before her, she sighed at the thought that there was no one to help her, no one to take an interest in her choice. Ruth was gone, and Virginia missed her sorely, feeling as if the loneliness, the uncongeniality of her home would be intolerable but for the thought of the release so soon coming. She felt that, though her little efforts in the village had had some reward, within doors she had never felt naturalized, never been able to produce any impression. Her father never showed her nearly as much affection as her uncle did, and she could not know how much this was owing to a sense of his own deficiencies towards her. He was exceedingly irritable, too, and difficult to deal with, discontented wholly with life; while Miss Seyton's sarcastic tongue always seemed to pierce the weak places in Virginia's armour, and when she was inclined to be cheerful, her talk implied such alien views of life and duty that she made Virginia wretched.

Dick had been offered some appointment in London, provided that he could pass a decent examination next spring, but his sister could not perceive that he made much preparation for it. She also began to suspect that he and Nettie Lester were more together than was good, and to wish for an opportunity of hinting as much to Cheriton, whom she instinctively felt to be the best depositary of such a vague suspicion.

But Cheriton was much less well again; he had been obliged to give up going to Paris, and the whole family were suffering anxiety on his account, more trying, perhaps, though less openly acknowledged, than that caused by his actual illness. Virginia was not quite the girl to deal successfully with her home troubles. Ruth, who did not care a bit whether she could respect her relations or not, had made herself more agreeable to them; while Virginia was timid and miserable, afraid of being unfilial, and yet perpetually conscious of defects. Of course, if she could have felt that Alvar had really comprehended her troubles, they would have weighed more lightly; but though his tenderness always made her forget them for a time, she never had the sense of taking counsel with him.

Now, as she turned over her patterns, her first thought was which he would prefer, and as her aunt came in and with irresistible feminine attraction began to examine them, Virginia said,—

"I shall wait till Alvar comes, and ask him whether he would like me to have silk or satin."

"He will tell you that you look enchanting in either. That will be a pretty compliment, and save the trouble of a choice."

"Oh, no," said Virginia, "Alvar has a great deal of taste, and he likes some of my dresses much better than others. I wonder if Cherry is better to-day."

"Probably, as I see his most devoted brother coming up the garden."

Virginia's face flushed into ecstasy in a moment. She sprang to the garden door, scattering her patterns on the floor; while her aunt looked after her, and muttered more softly than usual as she left the room, "Poor little thing!"

Alvar looked very grave as he came towards her, as if he hardly saw the slender figure in its fluttering delicate dress, or noticed the eager eyes and smiling lips; but, as usual, he smiled when he came up the steps, and seemed to put aside his previous thoughts, and to adopt the courteous manner which made Virginia feel herself held at a distance.

For once, she was more full of her own affairs than of his. "Look," she said, picking up her silks, "do you see these? Which do you like best?"

Alvar twisted the patterns over his fingers as he stood in the window and did not at once answer.

"How is Cherry?" she said. "Is he better to-day?"

"Perhaps—a little," said Alvar. "But the doctors have seen him again, and they say that he must not stay here—that he must go abroad for all the winter."

"Do they?" said Virginia; "that looks very serious."

"Ah yes," said Alvar a little impatiently, "but my father—they all talk as if it would kill him to go; he will get well away from these bitter winds—and—and the businesses that are too much for him."

"Yes," said Virginia slowly, perceiving that Alvar did not quite understand how

startling a sound being ordered abroad
had to English ears after such an illness
as Cheriton's. "What does he say himself about it?"

"He dreads it very much; but we will
go to Seville, and then he *must* find it
pleasant."

Virginia started; she changed colour,
and her heart began to beat very fast.

"*Mi querida!*" said Alvar, taking her
hand. "I feel that I—affront you—I do
not know how to ask you to let me go;
but how can I send my brother away
without me? For his sake I expose
myself perhaps to blame from your
father——"

"I don't quite understand," said Virginia, withdrawing a little, and speaking
with unusual clearness. "Did Cherry ask
you to go with him?" ·

"Ah, no. He refused and said it must
not be. But he told Jack that he hated
the thought of going to Mentone or any
such place alone. My father is too
unhappy about him to be his companion,

and Jack must go to Oxford. So, when I told him how the wish of my heart was to show him my Spanish home, he owned that he should like to see it. The climate will not cure him if he is dull and miserable."

"Certainly you must go with him," said Virginia steadily, though she felt half suffocated.

"Ah, *mi reyna!*" cried Alvar, his brow clearing; "you see my trouble. Without your approval 1 could not go!"

Virginia turned round and fixed her eyes on Alvar with a look never seen before under their soft fringes. The sharp agony of personal loss and disappointment, the feeling, horrible to the gentle modest girl, that the loss and the disappointment reserved all their sting for *her*, the outward necessity of the proposal, and the inward knowledge that Alvar wronged her by his feeling, though not by his act, drove her to bay at last. She would have *shared* in any sacrifice, but she instinctively knew that Alvar was making none. The vague dissatisfactions, the dim misunderstandings, the unacknowledged jealousies of many months, all rushed at once into the light. Her love was too passionate to be patient, and her self-control broke down at last.

"Yes," she said, "of course you must go with your brother. I see that. I admit it quite. But—Alvar—that's not all. I have seen for a long time that our engagement was a tie to you—it was a mistake. I don't blame you— you did not understand—but it is better to end it. I release you—you are free!"

"*Señorita!*" cried Alvar, flashing up, "I have given no one the right to doubt my honour. You mistake me."

"No," said Virginia, "I do not mistake. I know—I know you mean rightly—I ought not to wonder if you don't—if you don't——" she broke off faltering and trembling, humiliated by the sense that she had not been able to win him.

But Alvar's pride had taken fire. "I am at your service," he said proudly, "since you mistake my request."

" I will not hold you back one day," she answered. "Nor do I blame you. Don't mistake *me*. You have done all for me that you could ; but our ideas are different, and I feel convinced we should only go on making each other unhappy. It is better to part."

" Since it is your wish to have it so," said Alvar in a tone of deep offence, but with a curious pang at his heart. " I was your true lover, and I would never have caused you grief. But since I did not satisfy you, I withdraw. I force myself on no lady."

" Indeed—indeed," faltered Virginia, " I do not blame you ; it is perhaps my fault, that—that we have so often mistaken each other."

" It is that to you—as to my father I am a stranger," said Alvar. " I will go— it is as you wish."

He took up his hat, paused, made her a formal bow, and went out. Virginia sprang after him ; but he did not look back. She felt herself cruel, exacting, selfish, and yet she *knew* that her causes

of complaint were just. She had sent him
away from her, and she would never see
him again. As he passed out of sight,
she ran down the steps, whether after him
or away from the house, she hardly knew.
The trailing overgrown roses caught in her
dress and held her back. She turned, and
all the desolation of the untrimmed garden
and unpainted house seemed to overwhelm
her spirit. The wind came up in long,
dismal rustles, the sky was grey and cold.
As she paused, she saw her aunt's still
graceful figure in its shabby dress cross
the lawn, her face with its fair outline and
hard, bitter look turned towards her.

" *She* lost *her* lover ! " thought Virginia,
and her own future flashed upon her like a
dreadful vision. She turned and fled up to
her own room, where every other thought
was destroyed by the sense of loss and .
misery. It was in the middle of the
afternoon that she was startled out of
her trance of wretchedness by a call in
her aunt's voice, "Virginia, Virginia !
Come here, I want you particularly."

Virginia obeyed passively. She might as well tell her aunt of the morning's interview then as put it off longer. As she came into the drawing-room, Miss Seyton left it by another door, and she found her‑ self alone with Cheriton Lester.

" Thank you for coming down," he said, eagerly. " I want to explain; I think there has been a great mistake."

" No, I think not," said Virginia, rather faintly.

" But let me tell you. It is all my fault indeed. Alvar must not be punished for my selfishness. You know, I got a fresh cold somehow, and my cough was bad again, so my father was frightened and sent for the doctors, and they ordered me away for the winter. I must not go to London now, they say— "

" Indeed, Cherry, I am *very* sorry," faltered Virginia, as the cough stopped him.

" No, but let me tell you. This was a great shock to me. I want to get to work —and then—my poor father! It seemed to knock me down altogether, and foolishly,

I let Jack see it, and said that I hated the notion of any of those regular invalid places, and that going there would do me no good. And then Alvar came and asked me if I should not like to see his friends and Seville, and I said, ' Yes, if I must go anywhere,' and he tried in his kind way to make the idea seem pleasant to me, and my father caught at it because he thought I might like it. I shall never forgive myself for making such a fuss! But of course to-day—now I am in my right senses—I should not think of such a thing. If Alvar goes with me, even to Seville, and stays for a few weeks, then, if I am better, he can come home, and I shall not mind staying there alone, and at Christmas Jack might come to me, or my father—it can easily be managed. In short, Virginia," he added, with an attempt at his usual playfulness, " I want you to understand that I made a complete fool of myself yesterday, and that that's the whole of it."

" Did Alvar ask you to come and tell me this ? "

"No," said Cheriton, "he was hurt by your misunderstanding him, he does not know I am here. Jack drove me over. But I shall not agree to any other arrangement than what I have told you, unless," he added slowly, "things should go badly, and then I *know* you would have patience."

"Oh, Cherry," said Virginia, struggling with her tears, "I hope you don't think me so selfish as to wish to prevent Alvar from going with you. It is not *that.*"

"But what is it, then? Can you tell me?" said Cherry gently, and sitting down by her side.

"I have no one to ask," she said; "but you will think me wrong, and yet—"

"I know too well how difficult it is to be right in matters of feeling, if you once begin to analyze them," said Cherry sadly.

The gentleness of his voice and the kind look of his eyes gave her courage, and she said, very low,—

"I think I should not make Alvar happy,

because he does not care for me. Please
understand that he has done all he could;
he is very *kind* to me, but he does not
care for me."

"You know, Virginia," said Cherry
eagerly, "Alvar has different ways from
ours. Indeed, he *is* loving— "

" He loves *you*," said Virginia quickly;
then, blushing scarlet, she added, "oh,
Cherry, I think it is beautiful the way he
is grateful to you, and thinks so much of
you. Please, please, don't think I would
have it otherwise."

" I have far more cause to be grateful
to him."

"Yes! I like to think that. But
Cherry, when you were ill, he didn't care
for me to comfort him, it was no rest to
him to come and see me. He never tells
me his troubles. It isn't as Ruth and
Rupert love each other. If I say anything,
he turns it aside. It will not make him
unhappy to give me up."

" It made him exceedingly angry," said
Cheriton, too clear-sighted not to acquiesce

in the truth of Virginia's words, though he
was unwilling to own as much.

" I don't think," said Virginia, " that I
should bear that feeling patiently. Things
are very miserable any way, but I think
Alvar will be happier without me. It has
not turned out well."

She spoke in a low tone of complete
depression, evidently uttering convictions
that had been long formed, gently and
humbly, but with an undercurrent of
firmness.

" I will tell Alvar what you say," he
said. " I quite see what you mean, but
perhaps he will be able to show you that
you have misinterpreted him."

" No," said Virginia, with decision, " do
not let him try."

As she spoke, there was a tap at the
door, and Jack opened it.

" Cherry," he said, " it is so late; are
you ready ? "

" One minute, Jack," said Cheriton, " I
am coming. Virginia," he added, taking
her hands in his with sudden earnestness,

"Alvar will love you enough some day. I am sure of it."

Cheriton hardly knew what put the words into his mouth; but they chimed in Virginia's heart for many a weary day, lighted up by the bright, brave smile which had accompanied them.

CHAPTER XXV.

FAREWELL.

" O near ones, dear ones ! you in whose right hands
　　Our own rests calm, whose faithful hearts all day,
Wide open, wait till back from distant lands
　　Thought, the tired traveller, wends his homeward
　　way."

" OF course, since Miss Seyton insists, and
you say you wish it, I come home for my
marriage in October," said Alvar.

" You don't understand," replied Cheriton vehemently, " and you are unfair to
Virginia. She is as kind as she can be.
Go and show her that you really care for
her as she deserves, and it will all come
right. If anything could make matters
worse for me, it would be to think I had
been the excuse for a break between
you ! "

Alvar was standing in the library window, leaning back against the shutter. He looked perfectly unmoved and impervious to argument, his mouth shut firm and his eyebrows a little contracted. Cheriton, on the other hand, half lying on the window seat, was flushed and eager as if he had been pleading for himself, not for another.

"No," said Alvar obstinately. "Miss Seyton has dismissed me. She tells me that I do not content her. Well, then, I will go."

"Why make yourself wretched for a mere misunderstanding?"

"I? I shall not be wretched. I hope I can take my dismissal from a lady. She finds that I do not suit her, so I withdraw," said Alvar in a tone of indescribable haughtiness.

"Perhaps she knows best," said Cherry, "and is right in thinking you indifferent to her."

"No—but I will be so soon," said Alvar coolly.

"It is no good to *say* so," said Cherry; then, starting up, he came and put his hand on Alvar's arm. "Don't do this thing," he said imploringly, "you don't know what it will cost you."

The two faces clear against the sky were a contrast for a painter; Alvar's with its rich dark colouring, and calm impassive look just a little sullen, and Cheriton's delicate, sharpened outlines, the eyes all on fire and the colour varying with excitement.

Perhaps the two natures sympathized as little as the faces. Alvar's look softened, however, as he put Cherry back on the cushions.

"Lie still," he said; "why do you care so much? You will be as ill as you were yesterday. If I had known it, you should not have gone to Elderthwaite."

"But," said Cherry, more quietly, "I felt sure that there had been a misunderstanding. It was my fault. Of course I like best to have you with me; but I could not consent to any indefinite putting off of your marriage. My father would not agree to it either. And that is not quite the point. Show Virginia that she is your first thought, and everything can be put right."

Alvar stood silent for a minute, then said suddenly and emphatically,—

" No. I have not the honour of pleasing her as I am. I can change for no one. Do not grieve, *Cherito mio*, I shall forget all when I show you Seville, and I will teach you to forget too. I take the best of my English home with me when I take my brother."

He took Cheriton's hands in his as he spoke, with a gesture, half playful, half tender. The response was cruelly disappointing. Cherry withdrew a little and said, in a tone of extreme coldness,—

" In that case Virginia is perfectly right. I quite understand her meaning. But it will be a great vexation to my father that your engagement should be broken for such a cause."

" My father cannot complain. I have

obeyed him," said Alvar. "But I shall go and tell him that the proposals he so honourably made me will be unnecessary."

He went away as he spoke, and Jack, who had been listening silently, exclaimed,—

"By Jove! he doesn't know what he's in for now?"

"Oh," cried Cherry, "it is intolerable! If they had married, she would never have found out his coolness! It is most unlucky."

"Well," said Jack, "I don't know. Alvar worships you, and has ways that suit you, yet you can't understand each other. Alvar is altogether different from us. He is outside our planetary system, and always will be. I'd like my wife to belong to the same species as myself."

"But the occasion is so annoying," said Cherry. "Why must they order me off in this way—or why couldn't I have held my tongue about it? Oh, Alvar is the wise man after all."

"You'll get well," said Jack gruffly.

"Well, I'll try. But—," he paused; but the thought in his mind was that the home ties had regained their power now that he believed himself likely to leave them for ever.

"Cherry," said Jack, turning his back, and hunting in a bookshelf, "I know all about it."

"Do you, Jack?"

"Yes. You ought to go away; but do you mind going alone with Alvar? Let me come."

"Well, Jack," said Cheriton, after a pause, "if you know, I can tell you how it is. I've had a hard time, and I think I should like to be quiet. But it is right to give oneself a chance, and as for Alvar, I am not at all afraid of going alone with him. You know what a good nurse he is. *If* I want you, you will come to me."

"Yes," muttered Jack.

"But I don't want father to guess at what the doctors call 'mental anxiety,' nor to talk hopelessly to him. You must comfort him. I'm afraid a great deal will be thrown on you, my boy."

Jack did not answer; and Cheriton, divining his feelings, made an effort, and said cheerfully,—

"Of course, one is no judge oneself in such cases. I am quite willing to go now, and I shall look forward to seeing you at Christmas. You must write and give me your impressions of Oxford."

"Oh yes," said Jack, consoled; "and perhaps Alvar will pick up a Spanish lady, and then we should be all right again."

Cherry smiled and shook his head, feeling that he could not wish to dispose of Alvar in so unceremonious a fashion. He was angry with him now, and felt how wide a gulf lay between their points of view; yet he had grown to be very dependent on him, and was keenly conscious of all his unselfish devotion. He saw, too, that it would not do to talk freely even to Jack, since it frightened him and made him miserable, and resolved to keep all his confusing feelings to himself—feelings that seemed to tear him to pieces while he was utterly weary of them all.

He was afraid that he had been hard on

Alvar, and still more afraid of how his father would take the revelation; but he had long to wait before the study door was flung open, and Alvar walked in, with his head up, and his face crimson. He was passing through without heeding his brothers, but Cherry's call checked him, and he came up to the window.

"*Mi querido*, this will do you harm," he said gently; "you excite yourself too much."

"But tell me—"

"Yes, I will tell you. But we will go upstairs; you must rest."

But as he spoke, his father came out of the study, and coming up to them, said, in a tone of strong indignation,—

"I wish to know, Cheriton, how long you have been aware of a state of feeling on your brother's part which places me in a situation of which I am thoroughly ashamed; whether you were aware that, as appears from his own confession, *my* son has done Miss Seyton the disrespect of engaging himself to her as a matter of expediency, and not of affection."

"Sir," said Alvar firmly, "your displeasure is for me alone. I will not allow my brother to be questioned; he is not strong enough to bear it."

"No, Alvar, it won't hurt me. Father, I don't think you understand. If they find that they cannot satisfy each other, it is better to part. Neither would act dishonourably by the other."

"There is no use in talking," said Alvar hotly. "At my father's wish I gave myself to Miss Seyton as I am. Well, she rejects me; there is an end of it. I can change for no one. I am myself. Well, I do not please any of you, but I do not ask you to change yourselves, nor will I."

His words sounded like a mere defiance to his father, but as Cheriton heard them, he felt their force. Why should they all expect Alvar to conform to their standard instead of trying to understand his?

"Be that as it may," said Mr. Lester, "you have found an unworthy pretext. I am far from ungrateful for all your kindness to Cheriton, but it was fair on none of us to take the opportunity of his going abroad to put off your marriage. If you had had the manliness to say at once that your engagement was distasteful to you, we should have known how to act."

"I will not stay—I will not hear myself so insulted!" cried Alvar, with a sudden fury of passion, that flared high above his father's angry displeasure, startling both the brothers into an attempt to interfere.

"Father is mistaken," cried Jack; while Cheriton began to say,—

"Come into the study, father; I think I can explain—" when his words were stopped by a violent fit of coughing. Agitated and over-fatigued as he was, he could not check it, and the alarm was more effectual than any explanations could have been in silencing the quarrel.

Alvar sprang to his side in a moment, and sent Jack for remedies; while Mr Lester forgot everything but the one great anxiety and distress. The doctors had given a strong enough warning against the possible consequences of such excitement to make them all feel self-reproachful at having caused it; and the next words exchanged between the disputants were an entreaty from Mr. Lester to know if Alvar was alarmed, a gentle reassurance on Alvar's part, and a request, at once complied with, that his father would move out of sight, lest Cherry should attempt to renew the discussion.

It never was renewed. When Cherry recovered, he was too much exhausted to try to speak, or to think of Alvar in any light but of the one who knew best what was comfortable to him, and once more everything seemed indifferent to Mr. Lester beside the approaching parting. But though a quarrel was averted, there was much discomfort. Mrs. Lester took her son's view decidedly, and treated Alvar like a culprit, the only voice raised in his favour being Bob's, who observed unexpectedly " that he thought Alvar was quite right to do as he chose." Mr. Lester had an interview with Mr. Seyton, and probably made more than the *amende* expected from him, for the next day he received a note from Virginia :—

"DEAR MR. LESTER,—As I find from my father that you do not entirely understand the circumstances which have led to the breach of my engagement, I think it is due to your son to tell you that it was entirely my own doing, and that I have no cause of complaint against him. We parted, because I believe we are unsuited to each other, not because he in any way displeased me; certainly not because he very rightly wished to go abroad with Cheriton. I hope you will forgive me for saying this, and believe me,

"Yours very sincerely,

"VIRGINIA SEYTON."

Well meant as poor Virginia's letter was, it may be doubted whether it much enlightened Mr. Lester as to the point in question; but he showed it to Alvar, who read it with a deep blush, and said,—

"She is, as ever, generous—but—I am a stranger to her still."

Meanwhile, all the arrangements for the journey were being made. Cheriton received a warm invitation from Seville, and it was agreed, at his earnest request, that his father should remain behind at Oakby, but that Jack should go with him to Southampton, whence they were to go to Gibraltar by P. and O. steamer, the easiest way, it was thought, of making the journey: In London, Cheriton was to see a celebrated physician.

He went bravely and considerately through all the trying leave-takings and arrangements, taxing his strength to the uttermost, in the desire to leave nothing undone for any one. He put aside with a strong hand, that inner self which yet he could not conquer, with its passionate yearning, its bitter disappointment, its abiding sense of wrong; but it was there still, and gave at times the strangest sense of unreality, even to the pain of the partings, which was true pain nevertheless though he seemed to feel it through the others, rather than through himself. Perhaps the vehement Lester temperament was not a very sanguine one, for though they were told to be hopeful, they were all full of fear, and Cheriton himself hardly looked forward to a return, or, indeed, to anything but possible rest from the strain of making the best of himself, for he suffered very much, while all the vivid and appropriate sensations with which he had once looked out on life and death had died away.

He could hardly have borne it all but for Alvar's constant care and watchfulness, and for the ease given by his apparent absence of feeling, and for the soothing of his tender gentle ways, and yet though he clung to him with ever-increasing gratitude and affection, there was a curious sense of being apart from him.

Alvar, though he had too much tact to fret Cherry by opposition, had no sympathy with the innumerable interests, for each one of which he wished to provide, and thought his parting interviews with the young Flemings and with many another waste of strength and spirits. Cherry had

also to go through a trying conversation
with old Parson Seyton, who, between
anger on Virginia's account and grief on
Cheriton's, was difficult to deal with, entirely refusing to see Alvar, and more than
disposed to quarrel with Cherry for going
abroad with him. Even Mr. Ellesmere regarded Alvar's conduct with considerable
disapproval, though he would not mar his
relations with Cherry by a word.

Alvar said nothing and made no explanations, but he was exceedingly impatient of the strain on Cherry's fortitude
and cheerfulness, not seeing what the
memory of this sad time might one day be
to them all, and least of all appreciating
the value of that last Sunday's church-
going and Communion, which, much as it
tried both their feelings and their shy reserve, not one of the others, even Bob,
would for worlds have omitted. Yet, when
many an old servant and neighbour made
a point that day of following the example
of the squire and his children, Mr. Ellesmere thought the scene no small testimony

to the value of the lives, which, however
faulty and imperfect, had been led, though
at different levels, with a constant sense of
responsibility towards man and of looking
upwards to God.   Yes, and as something to
give thanks for, even while his heart swelled
at the thought that the best loved of those
tall fair-faced youths might never kneel in
Oakby Church again.

That same Sunday evening, Mr. Lester
was sitting alone in the library in the dusk,
sad enough at heart, when Cherry came
slowly in behind him, and leaned over
the back of his chair.

"Father," he said, "I've been thinking,
and I want to tell you something before I go."

"What is it, my boy?—don't stand—
here, sit here."

He pulled another chair towards his
own as he spoke, and Cherry sat down,
and said,—

"Father, I think I had rather you knew
as much as I ought to tell you; I don't
want to have any secret between us."

"Well, my boy?"

" And, besides, I heard you say that, if
you could have found any reason for my
being worse, you would be less anxious
about me. Well, it is not a reason exactly,
but I suppose it made me careless. I—I've
had a great trouble lately—a—a disappointment. It's over now—but it cost me
a good deal at the time. I can't tell you
any more about it; but I thought—after
all—I had rather you knew—*now !* "

Mr. Lester did not ask a single question.

" I never guessed this," he said, in a
tone of surprise; then, after a pause,
" Well, my dear boy, it's a great relief to
my mind."

Cherry nearly laughed, though his heart
was full enough.

" You need never imagine that it will
turn up again," he said, decidedly.

" Ah, well, Cherry, we've all had disappointments," said Mr. Lester, more cheerfully than he had spoken for some time;
" and I'm glad there's something to account
for your looks lately. You weren't strong

enough for vexations. You'll shake them
off with the change of scene. But, my
lad, don't go and make a fool of yourself
in the reaction."

Cherry was sufficiently acquainted with
his father's history to guess at the drift of
this warning; but he only shook his head and
smiled, and then there was a long silence.
Cherry leaned against the arm of his father's
chair, and, after a long-forgotten childish
fashion, began to finger the seals on his
watch-chain.

" These are the first things I remember,"
he said.

Mr. Lester passed his arm round him, as
when he had been a slim boy, standing by
his side; and though no other word was
spoken, and in the darkness there were
tears on both their faces, Cherry felt that
after such a drawing together, this worst of
all the partings was easier to bear.

PART III.

SEVILLE.

"Wo die Citronen blühn."

CHAPTER XXVI.

FIGHTING THE DRAGON.

"Does the road wind uphill all the way?
Yes, to the very end."

"So, papa, here we are, off at last! I can hardly believe it, and nothing left behind! Isn't it delightful? Such lovely weather and so many people! I wish we were going to India right away! I wonder how many of those people are good sailors."

"A very small proportion, my dear, in all probability."

"How I do like to look at people and imagine histories for them! And you cannot start for India without a sort of story; can you? As for you and me, *we're* just going to enjoy ourselves!"

The speaker looked capable of enjoying

herself and all around her. She was a girl of eighteen or nineteen, dressed in a tightly-fitting dark blue dress with a little black felt hat, very becoming to her small, slender shape, and dark glowing complexion. She had pretty features and very white teeth, which showed a little in her frequent smiles; dark hazel eyes, bright, clear, and penetrating; and curly wavy hair, as black as an English girl's can be. She had quick, decided movements, a clear, firm voice, and the sweetest laugh possible.

Among all the anxious, hurried, fidgety people on the deck she looked perfectly happy and at her ease—not careless, for a variety of small packages were neatly piled up beside her, but entirely content; for was not the desire of her heart in process of fulfilment? Ever since Elizabeth Stanforth, always appropriately called Gipsy, had been a little girl, she had delighted in sharing her father's expeditions when the great London artist sought new ideas, new models, or a cessation from ideas and models, in the enjoyment of natural beauty.

These expeditions had not hitherto been
long or frequent, for Gipsy was the eldest
of seven, and holiday trips away from the
old house at Kensington were generally
made in company with her mother and the
children, with occasional divergences of
Mr. Stanforth's.   Gipsy, too, was but newly
released from the thraldom of lessons and
classes, though a week once at the Lakes,
and another in Cornwall, had shown
Mr. Stanforth that she possessed various
requisites for a good traveller—a great
capacity for enjoyment and a great incapacity for being bored, good health, a
good appetite, and a good temper.

Therefore, when a long-cherished wish of
Mr. Stanforth's own was put in practice,
and he set out for a three months' tour in
search of the picturesque in Southern Spain,
he took Gipsy with him, and this warm,
sunshiny September morning found them
on the deck of a P. and O. steamer, just
about to leave Southampton on its way to
Gibraltar.

They had arrived on board early, and

were now watching the approach of their
fellow-passengers, the farewells and last
words passing between them and their
friends: Gipsy simply delighted with the
novelty of the scene, and her father watching it with a peculiarly acute and kindly
gaze of accurate observation.

Mr. Stanforth, with his slender figure
and dark beard, looked young enough to
be sometimes mistaken for his daughter's
elder brother; she resembled him in colouring and feature, but keen and sweet as her
bright eyes were, they had not looked out
long enough on life to have acquired the
thoughtful sympathetic expression that
gave to her father's face an unusual charm
—a look that seemed to tell of an insight
that reached beyond the artist's observation
of form and colour, or even of obvious
character, and penetrated the very thoughts
of the heart, not merely to note but to
understand them. Perhaps this was why
Mr. Stanforth's portraits were thought such
good likenesses, and why his original
designs never wanted for character and
expression.

He was not thinking purposely of anything but his holiday and his daughter, but the blue sky and bright sunshine of this unusually summer-like September helped his sense of enjoyment, and every face as it passed before him interested or amused him from the bright, fresh-faced schoolgirl just "finished," and looking forward through a few parting tears to incalculable possibilities in her unknown life, to the climate-worn official who had been bored during his leave at home, yet was far from regarding India as a paradise. Brides blushing and smiling, mothers with eyes and hearts sad for the children left at home, young lads with the world before them—the deck offered specimens of all these. Some were surrounded by groups of friends, but most of the sadder partings had been got over elsewhere, and the passengers were coming on board with a sense of relief, and minds chiefly full of their luggage and their state-rooms, their places at the table, and their chairs for the deck.

As Mr. Stanforth's eye travelled over

the various groups he observed two young
men sitting close together on one of the
benches at a little distance.   The one
nearest to him sat with his face turned
away towards his companion, a tall, power-
ful lad, with fair hair, and features of an
unusually fine and regular type, now pale
and half sullen with a pain evidently
almost beyond endurance.   The other's
hand lay on his knee, and he seemed to be
speaking, for the boy nodded and murmured a word or two occasionally. " That's
a bad parting," thought the artist; " I
wonder which is the traveller."

   " Look, papa," said Gipsy, " there's a
model for you ! Isn't that an uncommon
face ? "   She pointed out to him a tall, dark
young man, with a peculiar oval face of
olive tinting, who stood close to them
making   inquiries   of   some   officials.
" There's   a   distinguished   foreigner   for
you," she said.

   " Yes, a foreigner of course ; a very fine
fellow."

   Something restrained the kindly-natured

artist from drawing his daughter's attention
to the parting moments that were evidently
so painful; but the " distinguished foreigner," as the last minutes approached, drew
near to the pair and touched the lad on the
shoulder. He started up; the other rose
also and turned round, showing a face like
enough in type to suggest the closest kin-
ship, but white, thin, telling a tale of sickness as well as of present suffering. They
grasped each other's hands. Mr. Stanforth
involuntarily turned his eyes away, and in a
moment the lad pushed through the crowd,
evidently unseeing and unheeding, passed
close by them and knocked over all Gipsy's
bags, shawls, and bundles, pushed on, never
knowing what he had done, and turning,
gave one last look at his brother, who met
it with a beaming, resolute smile, and a
wave of the hand.

The olive-faced foreigner who had followed, saw the accident, and made a gesture of apology, then bid the boy farewell
with clasped hands and some rapidly-uttered
sentences, watching him over the side, and,

coming back to the Stanforths, hastily re-
placed the fallen articles.

"Pardon," he said, "my brother could
not see."

"Don't mention it; no harm done,"
said Mr. Stanforth kindly, as the young
man moved away, other groups came up
and separated them, and he was seen no
more till dinner time, when he appeared,
but without his companion.

In the intervals of making acquaintance
with her fellow-passengers and of beginning
the letter which was to tell her mother of
every event of their tour, Gipsy Stanforth
speculated as to how the "distinguished
foreigner" came to call such an unmis-
takable Englishman his brother.

The three days that the Lesters had
spent in London had been trying and
fatiguing. Judge Cheriton and his wife
had come up from the country to their town
house on purpose to receive them, but the
very kindness and interest which had
prompted them to inquire into all the
causes of Cheriton's illness, and to question

the prudence of some of the home measures had fretted both Cheriton and Jack, the latter being a little disposed to resent any interference. But the right of the Cheritons to a share in their nephews' affairs had always been admitted, and Mr. Lester, little as he felt himself able to bear the further strain, would hardly have let them go to London without him, but for his brother-in-law's assurance that they should not start till every arrangement had been made. The judge was surprised at the confidence reposed in Alvar, and though he had too much sense to try to shake it, had caused Mr. Lester to insist that they should be accompanied by a servant experienced in travelling and in illness, instead of the Oakby lad at first chosen— an arrangement which Cheriton secretly much disliked, though he acquiesced in it as sparing his father anxiety.

Judge Cheriton also undertook to give Mr. Lester a full report of the physician's opinion, which was not, on the whole, discouraging. He said that though the illness

had left manifest traces, and that he considered Cheriton in a critical state, there
was nothing to prevent entire recovery, of
which the winter abroad offered the best
chance; and if he wished to go to Southern
Spain, Spain it might be, as rest and change
were as much needed as climate. There
was no use in thinking of any profession
or occupation till the next summer. Some
overstrain had resulted in a complete
break-down, and the cough was part of the
mischief. Fatigue, cold, and anxiety were
all equally to be avoided, but as there was
no predisposition to any form of chest
disease in the family, they might look forward hopefully.

This verdict entirely consoled Alvar,
who, indeed, had never looked much beyond
the present, and brightened the anxious
hearts at Oakby, especially when accompanied by a note from Cherry himself,
which he had made Jack read to " see if it
was cheerful enough."

He and Jack clung to each other closely
during those last few days, and till they

parted, Cheriton never ceased to be the
one to uphold and to cheer ; but when Jack
was out of sight, he broke down utterly,
and while Alvar was beginning to make
acquaintance with the Stanforths, Cheriton
lay fighting hard with all the suffering
which he had so long held at bay. He
was not passive, though Alvar thought
him so, as he lay still and silent, unwilling to speak or be spoken to. He was
struggling actively, strenuously, with all
the force of a strong will against a passionate and rebellious nature. He was sufficiently
experienced in self-control, and unselfish
enough to have succeeded in behaving well
and courageously under his various troubles.
But Cherry's notions of self-conquest aimed
higher and went deeper. He would be
master of his own inmost soul, as well as
of his outward actions. His eyes were pure
enough to see as in a vision what was implied in saying honestly, " Thy Will be
done," and clear enough to know that he
could not say it ; while, on the other hand,
there was scarcely any form of wrath and

bitterness to which memory did not tempt
him. Why must he suffer in so many
ways? Perhaps the moments of softer
yearning for the lost love of his boyhood,
sad as they were, were the least painful
part of his suffering. The loss of health
and strength, and of the power of substi-
tuting some other aim in life for those
earlier and sweeter hopes, came as a separate, but to so active a person, an exceeding trial, while he was separated from all
the lesser interests which had the power
of custom over him, a power in his case
unusually strong; yet in these he felt lay
the hope of salvation, at least from those
intermittent waves of utter despondency
which made all alike worthless and blank.
Cheriton had all his life tried to choose
the better part, to follow his own higher
nature, and seek what was lovely and of
good report, had all his life looked up-
ward. Had he not done so, these present
temptations would have attacked him on a
far lower level, or, set apart as he was just
now from all outward action, he would

more probably not have recognized that he had a battle to fight at all. But to Cheriton it was given to see the issues of the battle that has been fought by all true saints, and perhaps by some sinners; and his chief mistake now was that he was young enough to think that, like the typical dragon fights of the old world, it could be won by one great struggle. This was his inner life, of which no one knew anything, save perhaps Jack, who was like-minded enough to guess something of it.

Alvar only saw that he was weak and weary, and suffering from a great reaction of mind and body. He was a very judicious companion, however, and after a day or two of repose succeeded in coaxing Cherry on to the deck; where the fresh air sent him to sleep on the cushions that Alvar had arranged for him, more quietly than for some time past.

When he opened his eyes, and began to look about him, it was with a refreshing sense of life and circumstances apart from himself and his perplexities. The blue sky, the dancing waves, the groups of people moving about, the unfamiliar sights and sounds amused him. He looked round for his brother, and presently discovered him sitting at a little distance, smoking his unfailing cigarette, and looking both comfortable and picturesque in the soft felt hat, which, though not especially unlike other people's, always had on him the effect of a costume. He was talking to a young lady, with an air of considerable animation and intimacy. She was knitting a gay-striped sock, the bright pins twinkling with the rapid movement of her fingers, and she laughed often, a particularly gay, musical laugh.

Alvar glanced round, and seeing that Cherry was awake, sprang up and came over to him.

" Ah, you have had quite a long sleep," he said.

" Have I ? I feel all the better for it. This is very comfortable. And pray who is the young lady with the knitting-needles ? "

" Why, that is Miss Stanforth. Did I
not tell you how kind they have been ?
You see, Jack nearly knocked her down,
and so we made acquaintance; and just
now I was teaching her some Spanish."

" Did Jack create a favourable impression by that mode of introduction ? "

" Why, yes," said Alvar, delighted at
hearing the shadow of a joke from Cherry;
" for I explained how it was that he was
in trouble, and they were interested at
hearing of you. Now you must have some
breakfast, and then perhaps you would
like to see them."

" Oh, no," said Cherry, " I don't feel up
to talking ; but I am glad you have some
one to amuse you."

However, Cherry began to be amused
himself by watching his brother. He felt
the relief of having nothing to do and no
one to think of, and as he lay looking on,
was surprised at perceiving how sociable
the stiff, reserved Alvar appeared to be,
how many little politenesses he performed,
and how gay and light-hearted he looked.

Evidently Mr. and Miss Stanforth were the most attractive party, though Alvar seemed on speaking terms with every one; and at last Cherry, seeing that he wished it, begged that Mr. Stanforth would come and speak to him, and their new acquaintance, having the tact to see that he was shy in his character of invalid, came and sat down beside him, and talked cheerfully on indifferent topics.

"And where are you bound for," he asked presently, "when you reach Gibraltar?"

"For Seville," said Cheriton; "Don Guzman de la Rosa, my brother's grandfather, lives there at this time of the year. He has a country place, too, I believe, for the summer. But Alvar thinks the journey would be too much for me yet. I hope not; he must want to be with his friends."

"My daughter and I," said Mr. Stanforth, "have some friends at Gibraltar, and they have recommended us to join them at a place on the coast, San José, I

think they called it. Afterwards our
dream has been to spend some weeks at
Seville. Can you tell us anything of ways
and means there, for we are trusting
entirely to fate and a guide-book?"

"I'm afraid," said Cherry, smiling,
"that I am trusting with equally implicit
faith in Alvar. I haven't asked many
questions. Alvar, can you tell Mr. Stanforth what he must do, and how he must
manage in Seville?"

"All I know is at his service," said
Alvar, sitting down at Cherry's feet;
"but he will, I hope, visit my grandfather,
who will be honoured by his coming. My
aunt, too, and my cousins would be proud
to show Miss Stanforth Seville."

"Oh, papa," exclaimed Gipsy impetuously, catching these words as she approached, "to know some Spaniards.
Then we should really see the country."

She broke off, blushing; and Alvar,
springing up, offered her a seat, and introduced her to his brother, while Mr.
Stanforth said,—

"Thank you, we could not refuse such a kind offer; but I want to make Seville my head-quarters, and make excursions from thence. What sort of inns have you? Are they pleasant for ladies?"

"Papa, you know we settled that I was not going to be a lady."

"Did we, my dear? I was not a party to that arrangement. You are not *quite* a gipsy yet, you know."

"There are inns," said Alvar, "but the best plan is to take a flat in what we call a ' *Casa de pupillos*,' a *pension*, I suppose. I know one. Dona Catalina, who keeps it, is an excellent lady, most devout, and she once received an English family, so she knows better how you like to eat and drink."

"I don't mean to eat and drink anything that is not Spanish," said Gipsy, laughing.

"Indeed," said Alvar, "you will not often find anything that is English. I sometimes fear that my brother will not like that."

"You have a lively remembrance of being

asked to eat oat-cake and porridge, and drink what we call sherry," said Cheriton.

"But I will not expect that you shall like things that are strange to you, *querido*," said Alvar, a speech that revealed a little of the family history to Mr. Stanforth's sharp eyes; while Gipsy said earnestly,—

"Oh, the strangeness is what I expect to enjoy."

A good deal more information of different kinds followed, and Cherry wondered at his own ignorance of Alvar's former surroundings.

"Why, I did not know that your cousins lived with you," he said.

"I did not speak much of Seville to *you*," said Alvar, with ever so slight an emphasis, the first reminder he had ever given that there had been one to whom he could talk freely.

"We were all too much occupied with teaching you about Westmoreland, and lately I think I have been too stupid to care. But you must give me some Spanish lessons soon."

"Have you been long in England?"
said Mr. Stanforth to Alvar.

" I came at Christmas. Ah, how cold
it was! The boys and Nettie laughed at
me because I did not like it. They ran out
into the snow without their hats that I
might feel ashamed of sitting by the fire,"
said Alvar quaintly.

" Ah, we were a set of terrible young
Philistines ! " said Cheriton. " Do you remember the snow man and the wrestling ?"

" I wish you could wrestle with me
now, my brother," said Alvar affectionately.

" That must be the effect of Spanish
sunshine, instead of Westmoreland snow;
and in the meantime we must not tire
you with talking," said Mr. Stanforth,
perceiving that Cherry hardly liked the
allusion. " Come, Gipsy, isn't it time for
one of the innumerable meals we have on
board ship ? "

" Oh, papa, I am sure you are always
ready for them," said Gipsy, following him.

Mr. Stanforth, on discovering more
clearly the whereabouts of Oakby, recol-

lected having visited Ashrigg some years
ago, when engaged on a portrait of some
member of Sir John Hubbard's family.
He perceived with some amusement that
Alvar attached no ideas to his name or to
his profession; and Cherry had scarcely
realized either, so that when the next
morning Mr. Stanforth came up to speak
to him, with a sketch-book in his hand, he
said, quite simply,—

"I see you have been drawing; may I
look?"

"If you will not think I have taken a
great liberty," said Mr. Stanforth, giving
him the book.

Cheriton laughed and exclaimed at one
or two exquisitely outlined likenesses of
their fellow-passengers, hitting off their
peculiarities with a touch, then admired a
little bit of blue sky and dancing wave,
with a pair of sea-gulls hanging white and
soft in the midst, while under were written
the lines,—

> " As though life's only call and care
> Were graceful motion."

"How lovely!" he said; "how wonderfully well you do it! Ah, that is Alvar—yes, you have caught that grave, graceful look exactly. Alvar is just like a walking picture; he can't be awkward."

"I am afraid I have not been so successful with Alvar's brother; but the contrast was irresistible," said Mr. Stanforth, as Cherry turned another page, and saw a sketch of himself lying on the deck, and Alvar, leaning over him, and pointing out something in the distance.

"That is just Alvar's look."

"You are a much more difficult subject than your brother," said Mr. Stanforth.

"I? I don't think I'm fit to sit for my picture. We tried in London to get a photograph taken; but it made me look worse than I am, so we did not send it home."

"You must let me try again. As an artist I may be forgiven for rejoicing in the chance of studying such a likeness beneath such a contrast as there is between you two. See, your faces are in the same mould; it is the colour, and still more the character, that differs."

"I think that may be true of more than our faces," said Cherry thoughtfully; "but I see what you mean, at least when I think of Jack, and we were alike when I was well. I will show you."

Here Cheriton caught sight of the name on the first page of the book, "Raymond Stanforth," looked at the drawings, and then at his new friend's face with a rush of comprehension.

"How stupid I have been!" he exclaimed, colouring. "I beg your pardon. Of course I ought to have guessed who it was at once. Pray don't think I am so ignorant as not to know your pictures. And I have been presuming to praise your sketches."

Mr. Stanforth laughed kindly.

"You must not leave off doing so now we have found each other out. Don't imagine that appreciation is not always pleasant."

"You have a great many admirers at

Oxford," said Cheriton, a little stiffly and shyly. " Some of the fellows prided themselves immensely on their appreciation of all sorts of modern art ; but I'm afraid I don't know very much about it."

" You employed your time, your brother tells me, to better purpose ? "

" I don't know. I thought so then. And it seemed more worth while to get a ride or pull on the river. I don't see what a fellow wants in his room but an armchair and a place for his books, and a good fire. One had better be out of doors when one isn't working. I don't care to have my rooms like a lady's drawing-room. But of course," he added apologetically, " I always like to go to the Academy and see the pictures."

Mr. Stanforth looked very much amused, but he was interested too. It is not uncommon in youth that considerable powers of mind may be exercised so entirely in one line, as to leave many fields of intelligence completely blank, and there were many points on which Cheriton simply accepted the code of his home, which, put into plain language, was, that study was study, and recreation out-of-door exercise of different kinds, intellectual amusements being regarded with suspicion. But there was much more than the boyish " Philistinism " of this last speech written on the face of the speaker, and Mr. Stanforth felt inclined to draw it out.

" What did you say you were going to show me ? " he said.

" I wanted you to see the rest of us ! " said Cherry. " Where is Alvar ? He would get my photograph case."

Alvar was near at hand, talking to Gipsy Stanforth and to some other ladies, and he soon brought Cheriton a little leather case which contained a long row of handsome Lesters, and ended with the favourite dogs and horses, and a view of the front door at Oakby, with Nettie holding Buffer on the back of one of the stone wolves.

" There is a ready-made picture," said Mr. Stanforth.

" My brother loves that little animal,"

said Alvar smiling, "he would like his picture better than that of any of us."

"I am sure some of our dogs are worth painting," said Cherry, "but Alvar does not appreciate Buffer's style."

And so, brightened by the fresh companionship and new scenes, the days slipped by, till Cheriton wished their sameness could continue for ever.

CHAPTER XXVII.

SAN JOSÉ.

"The lizard, with his shadow on the stone,
Rests like a shadow, and the cicala sleeps,
The purple flowers droop."

AT Gibraltar the new acquaintances parted, and Mr. Stanforth and his daughter went at once to join their friends at San José, with many hopes expressed of soon meeting at Seville; whither Cheriton, unwilling to detain Alvar from his friends, wished to go immediately. Mr. Stanforth's holiday was not an idle one. Every walk he took, every change of light and shade was a feast of new colour and form for him, to be perpetuated by sketches more or less elaborate, and the enjoyment of which was intense. But the pair of dissimilar brothers had afforded him interest of another kind, and it was with real pleasure that he thought of a renewal of the intercourse with them, which came about sooner than he had expected.

His friends, the Westons, were a brother and two sisters, lively people approaching middle age. Mr. Weston had a government appointment in Gibraltar, and his sisters lived with him. They were enterprising, cultivated women, and very fond of Gipsy Stanforth; who possessed that power of quick sympathetic interest which of all things makes a delightful companion. She was always finding " bits " and " effects " for her father, or suggesting subjects for his pencil; and she was almost equally pleased to hunt for flowers for the botanical Miss Weston, and to look out words in the dictionary for the literary one, who was translating a set of Spanish tales.

À propos of these, she related with much interest their acquaintance on board ship, describing the two Lesters with a *naïveté* that amused her friends, and prompted Miss Weston to say,—

"You seem to have been very fortunate in your travelling companions, Gipsy."

"Yes, we were. And it will be such an advantage to know a native family at Seville. That sounds as if they were heathens; but——I declare that *is* Don Alvar, buying oranges! Oh, I am so glad to see you! So you have come here after all."

"Yes. Cheriton was so ill at Gibraltar that it was plain that he could not bear the journey to Seville. It is cooler here, and he is a little better; but he can do nothing yet, and I am very unhappy. I do not know what to write to my father about him."

"Oh, I am sorry," said Gipsy warmly. "He seemed better on board. And this place is so lovely."

"Yes," said Alvar simply. "I could feel as if I was in heaven in the sunshine, and when I hear the voices of my home; but when he suffers, it darkens all. But I must go back to him."

"Papa will come and see you," said Gipsy; "and this is Miss Weston, with whom we are staying. Good-bye. I think your brother will be better when he has had a rest."

Gipsy's cheerful sympathy brightened Alvar, who had expected that Spanish sunshine would make a miraculous cure; but Cherry's cough had been worse since they came on shore, and his spirits had failed unaccountably just when Alvar had expected him to recover them.

Alvar had all along declared that it would be better to go by a Cadiz packet and thence by rail to Seville; but Mr. Lester believed in Peninsular and Oriental steamers, and in the English doctors and hotels of Gibraltar. But there the heat and glare were hateful to Cheriton, the servant they had brought proved more of a hindrance than a help, and Alvar thought himself fortunate in obtaining leave from some Gibraltar acquaintances to use their house at San José for a month, after which Cheriton might be better able to encounter the

strangers whom he really dreaded more
than the travelling. Certainly if change
was what Cherry had needed he had obtained it thoroughly. Nothing could well
have been more unlike Oakby than San
José, and when Cheriton had had a little
rest, had been teased by Mr. Stanforth for
comparing the marble-paved *patio* of the
house to the Alhambra at the Crystal
Palace, and, moved by the fortunate sympathy that had enabled him to "take a
fancy" to the kindly artist, had confided
to him that he was very homesick, and
longed for Jack, though he did not like
Alvar to know it, he brightened up and
grew rather stronger. He was soon able to
sit on the beach and try to learn Spanish,
insisting on understanding the construc-
tion of the language, and asking questions
sometimes rather puzzling to his tutor;
while Gipsy set up a rivalry with him as
to the number of words and phrases to be
acquired in a day, in which she generally
beat him hollow. Nor had he any real
want of appreciation of the new and beauti-

ful world around him, and Mr. Stanforth helped him to enjoy it. Life would be very dull but for the involuntary inclinations to acquaintance and friendship that brighten its ordinary course, and "fancies" are more often things to be thankful for than to put aside. This one roused Cheriton from the dulness that accompanies sorrow and sickness, and enabled him to turn at any rate the surface of his mind to fresh interests.

Mr. Stanforth, on the other hand, whose sympathy had been quickened by the practice of a most kindly life, found much to interest him in the bright, tender nature, evidently struggling under so heavy a cloud, and did not wonder at the affection with which the young man was obviously regarded—an affection made pathetic by the sad possibilities that were but too apparent.

Gipsy was on very friendly terms with both the brothers, and was a new specimen of girlhood for them. She was quite as clever and as well educated as either

Ruth or Virginia, and had been in the
habit of living with much more widely
cultivated people—people who talked, and
had something to talk about, so that she
had a great deal to say; while there was
a quaint matter-of-factness about her too,
and she talked art as simply as she would
have talked dress; and while she was very
much interested in the two young men,
she never troubled herself at all about
her relations towards them. She scolded
Cherry for walking too far, and discoursed
on the suitability of his appearance for
artistic purposes with equal simplicity;
fetched and carried for him, and triumphed
over his deficiencies in Spanish. She received Alvar's courtesies and compliments
with the greatest delight, and proceeded to
return them in kind, till she actually rendered him almost free and easy, and he
talked so much of her that Cheriton grew
half-frightened, unknowing that his own
remark, that he wished Nettie could know
so nice a girl as Miss Stanforth, had in-
spired Alvar with the notion that Ruth

might find a successor in La Zingara, as he called her. But Gipsy was perfectly unconscious, and was moreover carefully watched over by her father and her friends. By the end of the month Cheriton was able to undertake the journey to Seville, and the Stanforths proposed to start at the same time, but to go by a different route, which enabled them to see more of the country.

"But," said Gipsy, one evening when they were all together on the beach, "we *must* get to Seville in time for a bull-fight, and Don Alvar says there are none in the winter."

"But, Miss Stanforth," said Cherry, "*you* surely would not go to a bull-fight?"

"Wouldn't you?" said Gipsy mischievously.

"Well, yes—for once I think I should."

"You would not like it, Cherito," said Alvar.

"Don't you?" echoed Cherry, with a glance at Gipsy.

"Oh, yes; it is grand! When the

bull makes a rush one holds the breath, and then—it is a shout ! ''

" I suppose it is a wonderful spectacle," said Mr. Stanforth. " I hope to have a chance, but I think Gipsy will have to take it on trust."

" Jack desired me not to encourage them," said Cherry, " but I must own to a great curiosity about it."

" But I shall not let you go," said Alvar ; " it would tire you far too much ; and besides you are too tender-hearted. My brothers," he added to Mr. Stanforth, "cannot bear to see anything hurt, unless they hurt it themselves; then they do not mind."

" Of course," said Cherry, " there is an essential difference between incurring danger, or at least fatigue and exertion yourself, and sitting by to see other people incur it. I have no doubt it is a barbarous sort of thing, and there is something dreadful in the idea of a lady being present at it ; but it would be stupid, I think, to come away without seeing anything so characteristic."

" The Spanish ladies do not mind it, nor I," said Alvar, "any more than you mind killing your foxes, or your fish; but it is different for foreigners. They do not like to see the horses, though they are mostly worthless ones, torn in pieces. You would be ill, *querido*, you might faint."

"Nonsense," said Cherry. "I might hate it, but I should not be so soft as that."

"You do not know," said Alvar, evidently not disposed to yield. "Some day," with a glance at Gipsy, "I will tell you. You shot the old horse yourself for fear the coachman should hurt him—but it made you cry; and if a dog whines it grieves you."

" Old Star that I learnt to ride on ! " said Cherry indignantly. "What has that to do with it ? "

"And besides," resumed Alvar, perhaps a little wickedly, "bull-fights are usually on Sunday, and are quite as bad as billiards or the guitar, which you say in England are wrong."

" These are frightful imputations on you,

Cheriton," said Mr. Stanforth : "a tender
heart and too strict a sense of duty. No
wonder you are obstinate. But if what I
have read be true, a bull-fight is a hard
pull on our insular nerves sometimes, and
I doubt if you are in condition for one."

"I don't want to see a bull-ring at
Oakby," said Cherry; "but Alvar is mistaken if he thinks I should mind it more
than other people do. There is enough of
a sporting element, I suppose, to keep one
from dwelling on the details."

"I see, Mr. Lester," said Gipsy, "that
you don't believe in the rights of women."

"No, Miss Stanforth, I certainly don't.
I believe in my right to protect them from
what is unpleasant."

"But not to give them their own way!
Papa, don't look at me like that. *I* don't
want to go and see horses killed on a Sunday, if Mr. Lester does. But a bull-fight
—the national sport of Spain—and the
matadors who are so courageous—ah! it
makes such a difference the way things are
put."

"You must learn to look at the essentials, my dear. But now shall we have a last stroll to the point to see the sunset?"

"You need not tell Granny if I *do* go to the bull-fight," whispered Cherry, as Alvar helped him up, and gave him his arm across the rough shingles.

CHAPTER XXVIII.

SEVILLE.

"Golden fruit fresh plucked and ripe."

"AND now, my brother, you see Seville. At last I can show you my beautiful city!"

"Why—why, you never said it was like *this!*"

The Lesters had finally settled to go to Cadiz by sea, and thence by rail to Seville, again breaking their journey at Xeres. The Stanforths were making the journey across country; but Cheriton was not equal to long days on horseback, nor to risking the accommodations or no accommodations of the *ventas* and *posadas* (taverns and inns) where they might have to stop. He was quite ready, however, to be excited and patriotic as they passed through the famous waters of Trafalgar, and curious to taste sherry at Xeres, where it proved exceedingly bad. They arrived at Seville in the afternoon, and were driving from the station when Alvar interrupted Cherry's astonished contemplation of the scene with the foregoing remark.

" Ah, it pleases you ! " he said in a tone of satisfaction, as they passed under the Alcazar, the Moorish palace, with its wonderful relics of a bygone faith and power —the great cathedral, said to be " a religion in itself "—and saw the gay tints of the painted buildings, the picturesque turn of the streets, the infinite variety of colour and costume, and over all the pure blue of the sky and the glorious intensity of Southern sunlight.

Cheriton had no words to express his admiration, and only repeated,—

"You never told me that it was like this."

" You did not understand," said Alvar ; " and perhaps I did not know."

He did not show any emotion, but his face smoothed out into an expression of satisfaction and well-being, and he smiled with a little air of triumph at Cherry's ecstasies. This was what he had belong-ing to himself in the background all the time, when his relations had thought him so ignorant and inexperienced, and Alvar, like all the Lesters, valued himself on his own belongings.

They drove up to the door of a large house, painted in various colours, and with gaily-striped blinds and balconies; while through the ornamental iron gates they caught glimpses of the *patio*, gay with flowers.

Cheriton thought of the winter's night, the blazing fire, the shy, stiff greetings that had formed Alvar's first glimpse of Oakby. The great gates were opened, and as they came in a tall old man came forward, into whose arms Alvar threw himself with some vehement Spanish words of greeting; then, in a moment, he turned and drew Cheriton forward, saying, still in Spanish,—

"My grandfather, this is my dear brother."

Don Guzman de la Rosa bowed profoundly, and then shook hands with Cheriton, who contrived to understand his greeting and inquiry after his health, and to utter a few words in reply, feeling more shy than he had ever done in his life; but then he was at fault.

"My grandfather says you are like what our father was when he came here; that is true, is it not? And now come in."

Don Guzman showed the way into an inner room, which seemed dark after the brilliant *patio*, and was furnished much like an ordinary drawing-room; and here Cheriton was introduced to Dona Luisa Aviego, a middle-aged lady, Don Guzman's niece, and to two exceedingly pretty young girls, and a little girl, her daughters. He felt surprised at seeing them all in French fashions. Here also was their brother, Don Manoel, a tall, dark, solemn-looking young man, who exactly fulfilled Cheriton's idea of a Spaniard, and enabled him to understand Dona Luisa's remark that Alvar had grown into an Englishman. The old grandfather was like a picture of Don Quixote, a very ideal of chivalry, which character a life of prudent, careful indifferentism entirely belied.

Alvar would not let Cherry stay to talk, telling him that he must rest before dinner, which was at five, and soon took him upstairs into a very comfortable bedroom, looking out on a pretty garden, and opening into another belonging to himself.

Cheriton laughed and submitted, but the novelty and beauty had taken his impressionable nature by storm and carried him quite out of himself. When left alone, he had leisure for the surprising thought that his father had gone through all these experiences without their apparently leaving any trace except one of distaste and aversion; next, to wonder whether it was Alvar's fault or their own that they had remained so ignorant of Alvar's country; and lastly, that spite of the similarity of colouring to his Spanish kindred and something in the carriage, Alvar *did* look like a Lester and an Englishman after all.

Cherry had got used by this time in some degree to the Spanish eatables, and as he liked the universal chocolate and was as little fanciful as any one so much out of health could be, he got on as well as his bad appetite would let him, with the *ollas* and *gazpachos* spite of their garlic, and at any rate he liked omelettes and the bread, which was excellent. Their servant, Robertson, had, however, regarded everything Spanish with such horror, and had proved of so little use and so disagreeable, that Cheriton finally cut the knot by sending him back to Gibraltar, where he hoped to find a homeward-bound family, Alvar being certain that there would be sufficient attendance at his grandfather's.

Conversation at dinner was difficult. They all understood a little English, which was rather more available than Cheriton's Spanish, and Don Manoel spoke tolerably fluent French, to which, as Cheriton had in his time earned several French prizes, he *ought* to have been able to respond more readily than was perhaps the case. Cheri-

ton did not mind seeing grapes and melons
eaten after soup, though he thought the
taste an odd one, but he could not quite
reconcile himself to the universal smoking
after the first course in the presence of the
ladies. The young ones were very silent,
though they cast speaking glances at him
with their great languishing eyes; till after
dinner the little girl, whom Cherry thought
the softest and prettiest thing he had ever
seen, produced a great blushing and titter-
ing by whispering a question, which, while
apparently reproving, Dona Carmen was
evidently encouraging her to repeat to
Alvar, who sat on her other side.

Alvar laughed and shook his head.

" No, Dolores; I think there is not one
like him," he said, adding to Cherry—
" She wants to know if all Englishmen are
like you—white and golden like the saints
in the cathedral. It is true, she means the
painted statues."

" I am pale, because I have been ill," said
Cherry, in his best Spanish, and holding
out his hand. " Little one, will you make

friends ? What shall I say to her, Alvar ?"

But Dolores, with an ineffable expression of demure coquetry, retreated upon her sister, and would not accept his attentions, though she peeped at him under her long eye-lashes directly he turned away.

The family met at eleven for a sort of *déjeuner à la fourchette*, but every one had chocolate in their own rooms at any hour they pleased, with bread or sponge-cake, which they called *pan del Rey*. Alvar brought some on the next morning to Cheriton and while he was drinking it proceeded to enlighten him a little on the family affairs and habits.

" I perceive that the prayer-bell does not ring at half-past eight," said Cherry smiling.

" No, the ladies all go to church every morning. In the country my grandfather is up early, and Manoel too, but here I cannot say—we meet at eleven. It is usual to write letters or transact business in the morning on account of the heat."

"Does Don Manoel—is that what I ought
to call him ?—live here ?   Has he anything
to do ? "

Alvar then explained that Manoel had
no regular occupation, having a little money
of his own.   He smoked and played cards,
and went to the casino, " that is what you
call a club."   Moreover he was a very good
Catholic, and though he had not openly
joined the Carlist party—the Royalists as
Alvar called them—he was thought to have
a leaning towards them : but Don Guzman
never allowed politics to be discussed in
his house—neither politics nor religion.

" Is he a ' good Catholic,' too ? " asked
Cherry.

Alvar shrugged his shoulders.

" He conforms," he said.   " You understand that I am English.   I have no
part in these matters, otherwise at times
my grandfather might have suffered
for allowing me to be brought up as a
Protestant ; but I was taught to see that
they did not concern me.   But, *querido,*
you must not talk and ' discuss ' as you

do with Jack at home, or you might make a quarrel."

"No, I understand that. But if I were you I should not like to be supposed to be an outsider."

"In both countries?" said Alvar. "No; but you see I had been taught that I was an Englishman."

"Yet your grandfather would not let you come to England when you were a boy."

"My grandfather," said Alvar, "hates the priests. He would rather have me for his heir, though I am a heretic, than Manoel. That is true, though he would not say so. Look, he has seen many changes in this country, one is as bad as the other; he would rather be quiet and let things pass. So would I."

"The Vicar of Bray," murmured Cherry. "That creed is born of despair," he said aloud. "I should be miserable to think so of any country."

"Yes?" said Alvar, with a sort of unmoved inquiry in his tone. "You have convictions. In England they are not difficult. But, besides, my grandmother loved me very much, and not only was she religious like all women, she was what you call good. She would not part with me, and I loved *her*."

Alvar paused and put his hand across his eyes, with more emotion than he often showed.

" She thought," he continued, "that I should perhaps become a Catholic if I married a *Sevillana*, and that my father's neglect would make me altogether a De la Rosa. Forgive me, Cherito, it is not quite to be forgotten."

" I think it was very likely to be the case," said Cheriton.

" No, it was not the part for my father's son, nor for an Englishman, nor did my grandfather wish it. I am no Catholic— never ! "

" I suppose your tutor was—was a strong Protestant ? " said Cheriton, rather surprised at the first religious conviction he had ever heard from Alvar's lips.

"Well, I do not think you would have approved of him nor my father if he had known. He, what is it you say?—did no duty—and I do not think he was much like your Mr. Ellesmere. He told me that he was paid 'to put the English doctrines into me and teach me to speak English;' and he would say, 'Remember it is your part to be a Protestant because you are an English gentleman.'"

"But," said Cherry, "when you came to England you must surely have seen that we did not look on it in that way?"

"I did not much attend to your words on it," said Alvar. "As you know, what my father required of me I did, and I saw that English gentlemen thought much of their churches and their priests—or at least, that my father did so. I conformed, but I had not expected that in England, too, I should be a *foreigner*—a stranger. And I would not be other than my real self."

"I'm afraid we were very unkind to you."

"You? Never!" said Alvar.

"But why did you never tell me all this before? I should have understood you so much better."

"I did not think of it till I considered what would seem strange to you here —what you would not comprehend easily."

Cheriton remained silent. That Alvar had all his life considered himself so entirely as a Lester and an Englishman was a new light to him, and he could fully appreciate the check of finding himself regarded by the Lesters as an alien, for he knew that even he himself had never ceased so to look upon Alvar.

"We understand each other now," he said affectionately. "I am glad you have told me this. But, Alvar, though 'convictions' may seem to you easy in England, you would make a great mistake if you imagined that the religion of such a man as my father was for the sake of what you call conformity, and that it did not influence his life."

"No," said Alvar, "I did not think so of my father and you. I did not comprehend at first, but I see now that—it interests you."

"Never doubt that," said Cheriton earnestly. "You have seen all my failures, but never doubt that is the one thing 'interesting,' the one thing to—to give one another chance."

He paused as a look of unspeakable enthusiastic conviction passed over his face; then blushed intensely, and was silent. Like most young men, whatever their views, he was in the habit of talking a good deal of "theology," and could have rectified Alvar's hazy notions with ease; but personal experiences in such discussions were generally left on one side.

Alvar did not follow him; but perhaps that look made more impression than a great many arguments on the status of religion in England.

"Don't imagine I underrate your difficulties, or my own, or any one's," Cherry added hurriedly.

"I have no difficulties," said Alvar simply; "I believe you—always— Now, do not talk any longer—rest before you get up."

Cheriton now perceived that the sort of separation that had been pursued with regard to Alvar accounted for much of his indolence and indifference. He recognized how deeply his pride had been wounded by his kindred's cold reception, and he in a measure understood the sort of loyalty, half-proud, half-faithful, that held him to his own. He found that Alvar had never written a word of complaint of his family home to Seville; he perceived that as time went on he dropped nothing that he had acquired in England, either of dress or speech, attended the English service at the Consulate regularly, even if Cheriton was unable to go, and preferred to be called Mr. Lester. Cheriton saw that he intended no one to think that his English residence had been a failure.

But there was one phase of this feeling of which even Cheriton had no suspicion.

Alvar did not forget that one thing had belonged to him in England, to which Spain offered no parallel. He refused to answer any questions from his grandfather as to his engagement or its breach. He had not been brought up to think that romantic passion was a necessary accompaniment of a marriage engagement, but rather as a thing to be got through first; and it had been with a very quiet appreciation that he had given his hand away at his father's request. And when Virginia was once his, he was thoroughly contented with her, her rejection had wounded him exceedingly, and now he missed her confiding sweetness increasingly, he felt that a good thing was gone from him, and he would not now have attempted to console Cheriton as he had done at Oakby. But he never spoke of his feelings, and as Cheriton could not think that he had acted rightly by Virginia, the subject was never mentioned between them.

CHAPTER XXIX.

EL TORO.

" The ungentle sport that oft invites
 The Spanish maid and cheers the Spanish swain."

ONE of Alvar's first occupations was to
find a lodging for the Stanforths, and for
one of the Miss Westons, whom they
brought with them, and he succeeded in
obtaining a flat in a *casa de pupillos* or
pension, not far from the De la Rosa's, in
a picturesque street, with a pleasant shady
sitting-room, where Mr. Stanforth could
paint. There was a delightful landlady,
Senora Catalina, who went to mass with
the greatest regularity every morning, but
afterwards was ready to spend any part of
the day in escorting the ladies wherever
they wished to go, only objecting to

Gipsy's dislike to allow her dress to trail on the pavement, a point on which neither could convince the other, Spanish ladies considering the looping of the dress improper, and Gipsy not being able to reconcile herself to the normal condition of the pavements of Seville. Mr. Stanforth, however, frequently accompanied them, and they did a vast amount of sight-seeing, in which they were joined by the two Lesters so far as Cheriton's strength would permit; and as sketching often made Mr. Stanforth stationary, Cherry liked to sit by him, enjoying a great deal of discursive talk on things in general, and entering with vivid interest into the novelty and beauty around. Cherry asked a great many more questions about Moorish remains, and ecclesiastical customs, than Alvar was at all able to answer; and as his Spanish improved, endeavoured to pick the brains of every one with whom he came in contact; was so intelligent and so inquisitive about the arrangement of the different churches, that old Padre Tomè,

the ladies' confessor, looked upon him as a
possible convert, and though solemnly
warned by Alvar never to talk politics
with any one, could not always resist teasing him by hovering round the subject.
He got on very well with Don Guzman,
and listened to a great deal of prosing
about the best way of breeding young
bulls for the ring, and about all the
varieties of game to be found on the old
gentleman's country estate, and soon perceived that he had considerably underrated
the sporting capacities of the peninsula.
He was not a favourite with Don Manoel,
who suspected himself of being laughed at;
and though Dona Luisa was very kind to
him, he was hardly allowed to exchange a
word with the young ladies, and to his
great amusement perceived that he was
considered likely to follow his father's
example, and make love to them. Little
Dolores, however, was less in bondage to
propriety, and became very fond of him,
making vain endeavours to pronounce
" Cherry," and teaching him a great deal

of Spanish. Miss Weston, who was a hearty enthusiastic woman, with rather an overpowering amount of conversation, approved of what she called his spirit of inquiry, and was possibly not insensible to his good looks and winning manners. He did not now shrink from home letters, and indeed spent more time than Alvar thought good for him in replying to Jack's voluminous disquisitions on his first weeks of Oxford. Alvar thought that he had entirely recovered his spirits, and indeed Cheriton was one whose "mind had a thousand eyes," and they let in a good deal of surface light, though he was himself well aware of colder, darker depths whose sun had set for ever, and which could only be reached by the slowly penetrating rays of a far intenser light. Though no word of direct confidence ever passed between him and Mr. Stanforth, the latter knew perfectly well that mental as well as physical change had been sought in the sunny south. His health improved considerably, though with many ups and downs, he felt fairly well, and did not attempt to try the extent of his powers.

He was very anxious not to be a restraint on Alvar's intercourse with his friends or on his natural occupations; but except that he sometimes went to evening parties which Cheriton avoided, Alvar generally preferred escorting Gipsy and Miss Weston to the tops of all the buildings which Mr. Stanforth sketched from below, or into every corner of the Alcazar, and every chapel of the cathedral, both of which places had a wonderful charm for Cheriton.

Miss Stanforth was allowed to make friends with Alvar's cousins, Carmen and Isabel. She had once gone to a fancy ball, dressed in a mantilla, and had been told that she looked "very Spanish," with her dark eyes and hair; a delusion from which she awoke the first time she saw her new friends dressed for church (they did not wear mantillas often on secular occasions); and great was their amusement at Gipsy's vain endeavour to give exactly the becoming twist to the black lace, and to flirt her fan in the approved style. Gipsy was a bit of a mimic, but she could not satisfy herself or them.

"It is of no use, Miss Stanforth," said Cheriton, when she complained to him of her difficulties. "Alvar does not like walking out with me in an 'Ulster' when the wind is cold, so he endeavoured to teach me to wear one of those marvellous cloaks which they all throw about their shoulders; but I can only get it over my head, and under my feet, and everywhere that it ought not to be."

"Well," said Alvar, "you would not let me go to Hazelby in my cloak; you said that the little boys would laugh at me."

"But a great coat," said Cherry, "is a rational kind of garment that can't look odd anywhere."

"That is as you think," said Alvar; "but I do not care what you wear, if you like it. You will not certainly look like a Spaniard even in the cloak."

" A great coat," said Mr. Stanforth, " is one of those graceful garments which have commended themselves to all ages. I do not know what early tradition was followed by the inventors of Noah's Arks in the case of that patriarch—"

" Now, Mr. Stanforth, that is too hard," interrupted Cherry. " At least it has pockets."

" So many," said Alvar, " that what you want is always in another one."

" Alvar, that cloak is your one weakness. You clung to it in England, and you put it on the moment you landed in Spain."

" Cheriton thinks it is a seal-skin," said Mr. Stanforth smiling.

" Seal-skin," said Alvar. " No, it is cloth and silk."

" Did you never hear of the fisherman who married a mermaid, and she lived happily on shore till she fell in with a seal-skin ; when she put it on, and, forgetting her husband and children, jumped into the sea, and never came up any more ? "

" Ah, no ! " said Alvar. " It is only

that I want Cherry to be comfortable while
he is down among the fishes."

" I will take to it some day, for the sake
of astonishing Jack," said Cherry. " But,
Alvar, those friends of yours last night
were very much interested in my travelling
coat, and asked me if it was a Paris
fashion. They put it on, and I tried to
get Don Manoel into it; but he thought it
was a heretical sort of affair."

" Cherry, if you laugh at Manoel, he
will think you insult him. He hates
Englishmen, and our father especially.
He was angry because you gave the jessamine to Isabel—and—we are polite here to
each other; but if there is what you call
a row, it is worse than when every one is
sulky all at once at Oakby."

Cherry looked as if the temptation to
provoke this new experience was nearly
irresistible; but Alvar continued to Mr.
Stanforth,—

" I am glad that Cherito should laugh
once more as he used to do; but my cousin
does not understand."

"My dear Alvar, I will content myself
with laughing at you; you always understand a joke, don't you?"

"I do not care if I understand or no.
When I see you laughing," said Alvar
simply, "that is good."

Something in this speech so touched
Cheriton that his laughter softened away
into a very doubtful smile, and he changed
the subject; but he tried afterwards to
propitiate Don Manoel by the most courteous treatment. The Spaniard did not
respond, and he perceived that contending
elements were discordant in Seville as well
as in England.

Carmen and Isabel found novelty less
distasteful. It is true that they thought
Gipsy's free intercourse with their cousin
Alvar and with the English stranger
shocking; but they preferred them to any
other subject of conversation, and Isabel
in particular made quite a romance of the
incident of the Cape Jessamine, and how
Don Cherito had looked at her when he
gave it to her.

"But why shouldn't he pick a bit of jessamine for you, if you couldn't reach it for yourself?" asked Gipsy.

"Oh, Manoel said it was an attention."

"Oh dear no," said Gipsy, rather cruelly, "we shouldn't think anything of it in England. Don Manoel needn't be afraid."

"Oh, but Manoel is terrible. He swore before Don Cherito came that he would poniard us if we, like our Aunt Maria, listened to a heretic, a stranger. For Don Giraldo was a wild wicked Englishman, but beautiful in the extreme; they have no religion, and no morals."

"Isabel!"

"Ah, I tell you what Manoel says. He came, he pretended an accident, and then Dona Maria married him. Now, he says it is the same with Don Cherito. An illness—"

"Any one can see that Cheriton Lester is really ill, at any rate."

"Well—Manoel was angry with my grandfather for letting him come, and he has told Alvar that it should be death before such a marriage. Alvar told him he knew nothing of his English brother, who loved an English lady. But Manoel says that what happened once might again happen."

"Isabel," said her sister, "it is wrong to talk of this. If Zingara repeats it, there will be a quarrel."

"I shall not repeat it," said Gipsy; "but it is all nonsense, I assure you."

"Ah," said Isabel, "Manoel knows not. He knows not that I love one whom I have seen at mass, though I know not his name. But with my fan I can show him—"

"Isabel!" again said the grave Carmen; while Gipsy, who was far too well bred and well brought up to have made signs in church with anything, thought that "mass" and "a signal with a fan" sounded interesting, and that what would have been highly unladylike at home was rather romantic in Seville.

On their side, Carmen and Isabel thought Gipsy hardly used in being kept away from the bull fights, though she was too loyal to her nationality to express any wish to see them.

Don Manoel was a great lover of the ring, and as certain young bulls from Don Guzman's estate were to be brought forward at the last *corrida* of the season, there was a great desire that the Englishmen should be present. Mr. Stanforth intended to avail himself of the chance of seeing such a spectacle, and Cheriton, Don Guzman said, might see one contest, and go away before the other bulls were brought forward, if he found the fatigue too much for him. They would get seats on the shady side of the bull-ring, the great amphitheatre said to be capable of holding ten thousand spectators.

Cheriton, who went against Alvar's wish, did not stay for the end, and Mr. Stanforth went to see if he had repented of the rather perverse desire to prove himself capable of enduring the spectacle. He found him, still full of excitement, resting on a sofa in the *patio;* while Alvar sat near him, smoking, and looking cool and bored, as if the bull-fight had been a croquet party.

Mr. Stanforth's entrance was rather inopportune, for Cherry was still too full of his impressions not to talk of them, and, in answer to Mr. Stanforth's question, said eagerly,—

"Oh, the heat has tired me—that is nothing. But it made one feel like a fiend. I felt all the fascination of it—even the horror had a dreadful sort of attraction. I could not have come away if Alvar had not pulled me out when I was too dizzy to resist him."

"Very unwholesome fascination," said Mr. Stanforth.

"Unwholesome! I should think so! It is abominable that such things should be. I tell Alvar that in his place I never would encourage an appeal to the worst passions of human nature."

"Well, you would go, *mi caro*. I told you you would not like it," said Alvar coolly.

" You should set an example of indignation ! "

" I ? I do not care what they do to
amuse themselves. It does not interest
me, as much, I think, as it did you, my
brother."

" No," said Cherry slowly, " I understand a good many things by this. I
should be as bad as any of them. But
when a country encourages and allows such
' amusements,' when women look on and
like it, one cannot wonder at Spanish
cruelties. It appeals to everything that is
bad in one."

" You insult my country and your hosts !
Don Cherito, such language is unpardon-
able ! " exclaimed an unexpected voice;
and Don Manoel came suddenly forward
from one of the curtained doorways, close
at hand. " What right have you, señor,
to speak of our ancient customs in terms
like these ? "

" I beg your pardon," said Cheriton,
after a moment's pause of amazement, " if
I have said anything to annoy you; but—

I was not aware that you were present.
I was speaking to my brother."

" Would you insinuate that I disguised
my presence ? " cried the Spaniard, with
real rage in his tones, and a determination
to show it.

Then Alvar fired up with the sudden
passion that had always startled his English kindred.

" How dare you so address my brother !
He shall say what he chooses ! "

" He shall not — nor you either ! You
call yourself Spaniard — Andaluz — you
claim rights in Seville, and listen with com-
placence to the cowardly scruples—"

Here Alvar broke in with much too
rapid Spanish for the Englishmen to follow, interrupted as it was by Manoel's rejoinder, and by furious gestures as if the
disputants were going to fly at each other's
throats, while Mr. Stanforth's mild at-
tempts at interposing with —"Come—come
now ; what nonsense ! What is all this
about ? " were entirely unheard.

Meanwhile, Cheriton's previous excite-

ment cooled down completely. He got up
from the sofa, and stepped between them,
laying his hand on Alvar's arm.

" Excuse me, Alvar," he said, in his slow,
careful Spanish, " this seems to be my
affair. Señor Don Manoel, will you have
the goodness to tell me why you are
offended with me ? "

" He called you a coward—you, my
brother ! "

" My dear fellow, be quiet, don't be an
ass." (This in English for Alvar's benefit.) " Would you tell me what has pro-
voked you ? "

" Señor Don Cherito," said Manoel,
forced to answer civilly by Cheriton's coolness—" first, did you mean to insinuate
that I listened to your conversation with
my cousin ? "

" By no means," said Cherry. " I merely
meant to say that I had not seen you."

" Then I ask you, señor, to repeat or to
withdraw the remarks you made about the
bull-fight," said Don Manoel, with the air
of delivering an ultimatum.

"He will not withdraw them!" cried Alvar. "He is no coward!"

"I hope," said Cheriton, "I did nothing to offend. Were I in Don Manoel's place I should feel, I am sure, as he does. I, too, am attached to the customs of my country. It is no doubt difficult for a stranger to judge. If I said the sport was cruel, I did not for a moment mean to imply that—that—those who see it must be cruel. Excuse my bad Spanish. I cannot express myself, but—pray let us shake hands."

He smiled, and held out his hand.

"Well, señor, you are Don Guzman de la Rosa's guest. If this is meant for an apology—"

"For having offended you—yes. Being Don Guzman's guest, I could not quarrel with his nephew."

"I accept the apology," said Don Manoel, with much solemnity, and accepting Cherry's hand.

"But," said Alvar, "you applied an expression to my brother."

"Oh, nonsense, Alvar; you know we

never think of 'expressions' when we are
angry; and I'm not aware of having
had any opportunity of showing either
cowardice or courage."

" H'm," said Mr. Stanforth, in English,
" a tolerably cool head, I think."

Don Manoel, who appeared to have made
up his mind to be magnanimous, remarked
that his expression had been used too
hastily to a stranger; but that a true
Spaniard would look on any scene with equa-
nimity. Cherry's lip curved a little, as if he
thought this a doubtful advantage; but he
answered with a laugh,—

" I *am* a stranger, señor; and besides,
I was fatigued."

" Ah," said Manoel, " that amounts to
an entire excuse. The expression is with-
drawn."

And with a profound bow to Cheriton, he
went away, and Cherry burst out laughing.

" What in the world did all that mean?"
he said. " Did I really offend his national
pride by turning sick at the dying
horses?"

"That is not all," said Alvar hurriedly;
"he hates the English and us all; he
would like to kill me."

"Ah, ha, Alvar, it is my turn to talk
about 'excitement' now."

"Well, I do not understand you. When
you came home you could not be still;
you seemed crazy. And now, when any
gentleman would be enraged, you laugh."

"Oh, I hate quarrels. And besides,"
shrugging his shoulders, "why in the
world should I care for such mock-heroics
as that?"

"Ah, Cherry," said Mr. Stanforth,
"there spoke the very essence of English
scorn."

Cheriton coloured.

"True," he said, candidly, "Don
Manoel had a right to be angry with
me, after all. But I don't mean it. I
dare say he isn't half a bad fellow."

"Ah, you are coughing. You will be
tired out; and I am sure that you will not
sleep," said Alvar. "Come, you shall not
talk any more about anything."

" Very wise advice," said Mr. Stanforth, " especially as Gipsy has persuaded the whole party to come to-morrow to see my sketches, and drink English ' afternoon tea.' So rest now in preparation."

Cheriton paid for his day's work by a bad night and much weariness. Don Manoel made very polite inquiries after him ; but there was something in the atmosphere that, to quote Alvar, Cherry " did not understand."

CHAPTER XXX.

NETTIE AT BAY.

" A child, and vain."

AFTER the departure of the travellers, a period of exceeding flatness and dulness settled down on Oakby and its neighbourhood. The weather was dismal, one or two other neighbouring families were away, and no one thought it worth while to do anything. Jack had refused a congenial invitation, and conscientiously stayed at home " to make it cheerful," until he went up to Oxford; but, though he was too well conducted and successful not to be a satisfactory son, he and his father were not congenial, and never could think of anything to say to each other. He had outgrown companionship with

Bob, and did not now get on very well
with him; while Nettie was never sociable
with any one but her twin. Mrs. Lester,
though very attentive to her son's dinners
and other comforts, did not trouble herself
much about the boys, and moreover did
not possess the comfortable characteristic
common to most elderly ladies—of being
often to be found in one place. As Jack
expressed it to himself, " no one was ever
anywhere; " and prone as he was to look
on the dark side of things, the thought
that this was what home would be without
Cherry, was perpetually before his mind.
He did not like to go to Elderthwaite, and
saw nothing of its inhabitants till one
misty day early in October, as he was
walking through the lanes with Rolla and
Buffer at his heels, he came suddenly upon
Virginia, leaning over a stile, and looking,
not at the view, for there was none, but at
the mist and the distant rain. Her figure,
in its long waterproof cloak, under an arch
of brown and yellow hazel boughs, had an
indescribably forlorn aspect; but Jack,

awkward fellow, was conscious of nothing but a sense of embarrassment and doubt what to say. She started and coloured up, but with greater self-possession spoke to him, and held out her hand.

" How d'ye do ? " said Jack. " Down, Buffer, you're all over mud."

" Oh, never mind, I don't care, dear little fellow ! " exclaimed Virginia, who would have hugged Buffer, mud and all, but for very shame. " I did not know you were at home, Jack."

" Yes, but I'm going to Oxford next week."

" And—and you have good accounts of Cherry ? "

" Yes, pretty good, better than at first. He says that he looks better, and does not cough so much, and he likes it,—so he says, at least," replied Jack, who, conceiving that propriety precluded the mention of Alvar's name, found his personal pronouns puzzling.

" I am *very* glad," said Virginia softly.

" Yes, I suppose they are at Seville by

this time; they stayed at San José till Cherry was stronger. Al—he—they thought it best."

"Your eldest brother would be very careful of him, I am sure," said Virginia, with a gentle dignity that reassured Jack, though she blushed deeply.

" Yes," he said more freely, " and they have made some friends; Mr. Stanforth, the artist, you know, and his daughter; they're very nice people, and they have been learning Spanish together. He writes in *very* good spirits," concluded Jack viciously, and referring to Cherry, though poor Virginia's imagination supplied another antecedent.

" I am glad to hear it," she said. " I met that Miss Stanforth once. She was a pretty, dark-eyed child then. Good-bye, Jack, I am going soon to stay with my cousin Ruth."

" Good-bye," said Jack, with a scowl which she could not account for. " I hope you'll enjoy yourself."

" Good-bye ; good-bye, Buffer."

Jack took his way home through the wet shrubberies. He felt sorry for Virginia, whom he regarded as injured by Alvar, but he thought that she ought to be angry with Ruth, never supposing that the latter's delinquencies were unknown to her.

As he walked on he passed by a cart shed belonging to a small farm of his father's above which was a hay loft, reached by a step ladder, to the foot of which Buffer and Rolla both rushed, barking rapturously, and trying to get up the ladder.

"Hullo! what's up?—rats, I suppose," thought Jack; and mounting two or three steps of the very rickety ladder, he looked into the loft, his chin on a level with the floor. Suddenly a blinding heap of hay was flung over his head; there was a scuffle and a rush, and Jack freed himself from the hay to find his head in Nettie's very vigorous embrace; and to see Dick Seyton swing himself down from the window of the loft and run away.

"Stop, I say. Nettie, let go, what are

you doing here? Dick, stop, I say," cried Jack, scrambling up the ladder and rushing to the window; but Dick had vanished.

"Don't stamp, Jack, you'll come through; you should have run after him," said Nettie saucily.

Jack turned, but caught his foot in a hole and fell headlong into the hay, while Nettie sat and laughed at him, and the dogs howled at the foot of the ladder.

Jack picked himself up cautiously, and sitting down on the hay, for there was hardly room for him to stand upright, said severely,—

"Now, Nettie, what is the meaning of this?"

"The meaning of what?"

"Of your being here with Dick. I told you in the summer that I didn't approve of your being so friendly with him, and now I insist on knowing at once what you were doing with him."

"Well, then, I shan't tell you," said Nettie coolly.

" I say you shall. I couldn't have believed that my sister would be so unladylike. Just tell me how often you have
met him, and what you were doing here ?"

"It's no business of yours," said
Nettie, making a sudden rush at the
ladder; but Jack caught her, and a
struggle ensued, in which of course he
had the upper hand, though she was
strong enough to make a considerable
resistance; and he felt the absurdity of
fighting with her as if she were a naughty
child, when her offence was of such a nature.

" Now, Nettie," he said, in a tone that
she could not resist. " Stop this nonsense. I mean to have an answer. What
has induced you to meet Dick Seyton in
secret, and how often have you done so ?
You can't deny that you have."

" No," said Nettie, " I have, often, and
I shall ever so many times more."

" I couldn't have believed it of you,
Nettie," said Jack, so seriously and so
mildly that Nettie looked quite frightened,
and then exclaimed,—

" Jack, if you dare to venture to think that I meet Dick that we may make love to each other, or any nonsense of that kind, I'll—I'll kill you—I'll never speak to you again, *never !* "

" Why—why what else can I think ? " said Jack, blushing, and by far the more shamefaced of the two.

" Well, then, it's abominable and shameful of you. Do you think I would be so horrid ? As if I ever meant to marry any one. I shall live with Bob."

" Don't be so violent, Nettie. You have acted very deceitfully."

" Deceitfully ! Do you think I'd tell you a story ?"

As Nettie had never been known to "tell a story " in her life, Jack could not say that he thought she would; but he replied,—

" You *have* acted deceitfully. You have run after Dick when we all thought you were somewhere else, and—there's no use in being in a passion—but what do you suppose any one would think of a girl who behaved in such a manner ? "

Nettie blushed, but answered,—

" I can't help what any one thinks, Jack. I know I'm right, and I must go on doing it."

" Indeed you won't," said Jack angrily; " for unless you promise never to meet him any more, I shall tell father at once that I found you here. What do you think Cherry would say to you ? "

" Cherry would say I was perfectly right, and would do *exactly* the same thing himself," said Nettie, triumphantly. " I am not doing any harm ; and I must go on. I can't tell you why I am doing it, because I promised not, and I'll do it nearer home if you like it better. Bob and I quarrelled about it many a time, *he* knows."

" Oh, he knows, does he ? What a fool he must have been to let you do it."

" He won't tell of me," said Nettie, " and he never did let me when he was at home. But I am not a silly, horrid girl, Jack, whatever you think ; and I'm not flirting with Dick, nor—nor—engaged to him ; and when—when—it's right, I don't mind people thinking so ! "

But this speech ended in a flood of tears, as poor Nettie's latent maidenliness began to assert itself.

"And pray," said Jack, "does Dick come after you because it's right?"

"No—no," sobbed Nettie; "because I make him."

"And how can you *make* him, I should like to know?"

Nettie made no answer but renewed tears. At last she sobbed out "Oh, Jack, Jack, I wish you were Cherry!"

"I wish I were with all my heart," said Jack. "Would you tell me if I were Cherry?"

"No; but I know *he* would be kind, and not think me horrid."

"Well, Nettie, I'll try to be kind; but you frighten me by all this. Now just listen. I believe I ought to tell father directly."

"Oh, Jack! dear Jack! Don't, [don't —it would be dreadful! Don't you believe me?"

"Yes," said Jack, "I believe you; but

how do I know about a young scamp like
Dick? You tell me the whole truth, and
then I can judge, or I shall tell my father
this moment. You're my sister, and I
shall take care of you. You've done a
thing that may be told against you all your
life, and nothing can make it right, say
what you will."

"But I *can't* tell you, Jack; I've promised."

"Well, then, I shall have it out first
with Dick."

"Oh, Jack, everything will be undone
then!"

"And pray, if you don't care about him,
why does it matter to you so much about
him?"

"Indeed—indeed, Jack, I'm not in love
with him in the least. I never was with
anybody, and I never mean to be," said
Nettie, fixing her great blue eyes full on
Jack, and speaking with convincing eagerness.

"And how about him?" said Jack
crossly.

" No, it's nothing to do with it," said
Nettie; but the tone of her voice altered
a little, and Jack had a sort of feeling
that there was more in the matter than
she herself knew, for he never thought of
disbelieving her.

" Will you tell, and will you promise ? "
he said.

" No, I won't," said Nettie.

" Then you are a very naughty, dis-
obedient girl, and you shall come home
with me this minute."

" I hate you, Jack. I'll never forgive
you," said Nettie passionately, as she
followed him; and all the way home she
sobbed and pouted, with an intolerable
sense of shame, while Jack, utterly puzzled,
walked by her side, a desire to horsewhip
Dick Seyton contending in his mind with
a dread of making a row.

They came in by the back-door, and
Nettie rushed upstairs at once ; while Jack,
virtuous and resolute, went into the study.

Resolute as the girl was, she listened
trembling, till her father's loud call of

"Nettie, Nettie, come here this moment!"
brought her down to the study, where were
her father, her grandmother, and Jack.

"Eh, what's all this, Nettie?" said Mr.
Lester. "I can't have you running about
the country with young Seyton. What's
the meaning of it?"

"Papa," said Nettie, "I haven't run
about the country. Dick and I have got
a secret; it's a very good secret."

"Well, what is it, then?" said her
father.

"I don't mean to tell. I never tell
secrets," said Nettie, with determination.
"We have had it a long time."

"My dear," said Mr. Lester, much more
mildly than he would have spoken to any
of his boys, "I must put an end to it.
You have been running wild with your
brothers till you forget how big a girl you
are getting. Never go out with Dick
again by yourself—do you hear?"

Nettie made no answer, and her father
continued, more sternly,—

"I am sorry, Nettie, that you did not

know better how to behave. Never let me hear of such a thing again."

Still silence; and Jack said,—

" She won't promise. I shall see what Dick says about it."

" Then you'll just do nothing of the sort, Jack," said his grandmother, " making mountains out of mole-hills. Nettie is going to London to stay with her aunt Cheriton, and have some music and French lessons with Dolly and Kate. I'd settled it all this morning. She doesn't attend enough to her studies here. You'll take her up when you go to Oxford, and there'll be an end of the matter."

" Yes, yes," said Mr. Lester. " Grandmamma and I were talking it over just now."

" Not that it is on account of your remarks, Jack," said Mrs. Lester. " That would be making far too much of her foolish behaviour; but in London she'll learn better."

" To be sure," said Mr. Lester, who had been stopped on his way out riding by

Jack's appeal, and was now glad to escape from an unpleasant discussion. "Nettie will come back at Christmas, and we shall hear no more of such childish tricks."

Nettie looked like a statue, and never spoke a word; but there was a look of fright through all her sullenness. Jack was not accustomed to think much of her appearance, but he knew as a matter of fact that she was handsome, and it struck him forcibly that she looked "grown-up."

"You've done more harm than you know," she said; "but I will not tell, and I will not promise." And with a sort of dignity in her air, she walked out of the room.

"What does she mean?" said Jack.

"Never you mind," said his grandmother, "and don't you raise the countryside on her by saying a word to Dick or any one. Hold your tongue, and be thankful. The Seytons are the plague of the place, and we'll ask them all to dinner before Nettie goes, Dick included."

" Ask them to dinner ? " said Jack.

" Yes ; we'll have no talk of a quarrel. And besides, your father finds that people are apt to think that it was Virginia's fault that your half-brother left her in the lurch ; and that's not so, though she *is* a Seyton."

" No, indeed ! "

" So my son means to have a dinner-party, and to show that we are all good friends, and pay them proper attention. A bad lot they are ; there's not one of them to be trusted."

" But, Granny," said Jack anxiously, " what do you think about Nettie ? What secret can she have ? "

" Eh, I can't tell. He may be getting her a puppy or a creature of some kind ; but Nettie's secret may be one and Dick's another. I always blamed Cherry for encouraging the Seytons about the place."

" Poor Cherry ! " muttered Jack to himself, with a great longing to throw the burden of his difficulty on to Cherry's shoulders.

Nettie remained sullen and impenetrable. She treated Jack with an intense resentment that vexed him more than he could have supposed. Neither her father nor her grandmother asked her any questions; but she was watched, though not palpably in disgrace, and she suffered from an agony of shame and of self-reproach which contended strangely with the motive that in her view justified the stolen meetings. Whether her womanly instincts, roughly awakened, justified the warnings given her, or whether, she merely resented the unjust suspicion, she herself scarcely knew, and not for worlds would she have explained her feelings. The dread of giving an advantage, the intense sulky self-respect that leads to an exaggeration of reserve and false shame, was in her nature as in that of all the Lesters, and if Cheriton had been present she could not probably have uttered a word to him. Being absent, she could venture to soften at the thought of him, and cried for him many a time in secret.

CHAPTER XXXI.

BROKEN LINKS.

"Love is made a vague regret."

VIRGINIA, when she parted from Jack, walked slowly homewards through the mist and the falling leaves, and thought of the bloom and the brightness of that fair Seville which she had so often pictured to herself. How happy the two brothers would be there together, among all the surroundings which she had heard described so often! Alvar would never think of her. "At least, I should have had letters from him if I had not sent him away," she thought; and though she did not regret the parting in the sense of blaming herself for it, she felt in her utter desolation as if she had rather have had her lover cold and indifferent than not have him at all.

For life was so dreary, home so wretched, and Virginia could not mend it. Indeed in many ways a less high-minded girl with stronger spirits and more tact might have been far more useful there. Virginia held her tongue resolutely; but she could not shut her eyes. She had lost her bearings, and could not possibly understand the proportion of things. Thus even in her inmost soul she never blamed her father for his life-long extravagance, for the vague stories of his dissipated youth— these things were not for her to judge; but the conversation, which he intended to be perfectly fit for her ears, was full of small prejudices, small injustices, and trifles taken for granted that grated on her every hour. She tried very hard to be gentle and pleasant to her aunt; but she could not bring herself, as Ruth could, to laugh at scandalous stories, old or new, or even to think herself right in listening to them. And though her father and aunt *so far as they knew how*, respected her innocence, the latter only laughed at the ignorance that thought one thing as bad as another. For there *were* virtues, or at least self-denials in their lives, for which, with all her love and with all her charity, she could not possibly credit them. It was something that Mr. Seyton had pulled through without utterly succumbing to debt and difficulty, it was something that when writhing under an injury which she never forgot or forgave, his sister stuck to him and kept things as straight as they were. It was a godless, idle, aimless household, above stairs and below; but it was not a scandalous one, and, with all the antecedents, it easily might have been. But the obvious outcome of this hard narrow life was a deadness to all outer or higher interests, an ignorance of the ordinary views of society, and of modern.forms of thought never attained save by selfish people, an absence of restraint of temper, a delight in utter littleness, which were intensely wearying. Higher principles

would have made life more interesting if
nothing more. The narrowest form of
belief in religion and goodness would have
given a wider outlook. Virginia was sick to
death of tales of little local incidents spiced
with ill-nature, or incessant complaints
of some one's ill-behaviour about a fence or
a cow. If she had lived at Oakby she
would have heard a good deal of the same
sort of thing; but there there would have
been something else to fall back on, and
she would not have heard small triumphs
over small overreaching, which Mr. Seyton
did not mix enough with his kind to hear
commented on.

Virginia used to wonder if she would
grow like her aunt, her life was so empty.
All her young-lady interests, the essay and
drawing clubs, the correspondence and the
art needlework, with which like other girls
she had amused herself, had languished
entirely during her engagement, and she
did not care to resume them. She would
have liked to be a resource to Dick; but
she was not used to boys, and had not

much faculty for amusing them, and Dick
did not care for her. Her Sunday class
tired her, and were naughty because her
teaching was languid ; the children by no
means offering the consolations to her depression which they are sometimes represented
as doing in fiction. The Ellesmeres, who
were always kind to her, were away for
their annual holiday, and the library books
for which she subscribed, and which might
have amused her, could never. by any
chance be fetched from the station when
she wanted them.

Her uncle showed his sympathy by
scolding her roundly for fretting for a
black-eyed foreigner, till she was almost
too angry to speak to him.

Under all these circumstances Ruth's
urgent invitation had been welcome, and
as she received others from her friends at
Littleton, she resolved to go and try to
pick up the threads that Alvar had broken.
Soon after she parted with Jack she met the
Parson, and told him what she knew would
be welcome news, that Cherry was better.

"Ay," said Mr. Seyton, "Jack brought me a message from him that he would write me an account of a bull-fight. Wonder he's not ashamed to go near one. Cruel, unmanly sport—disgraceful!"

"Well, uncle," said Virginia, "I think you ought to be pleased that Cherry is well enough to go."

"Eh? I'll ask him if he'll come and see a cock-fight when he comes home. Plenty of 'em here—round the corner. So you're going to London to get a little colour in your cheeks, I think it's time."

"Yes, uncle; Mrs. Clement will teach the children while I'm away."

"Very well, and tell Miss Ruth she was blind of one eye when she made her choice, but *I* can see out of both."

"Uncle, I shouldn't think of telling her such a thing. What do you mean?"

"Never mind, she'll understand me. Good-bye, my dear, and never mind the Frenchman."

Virginia smiled, but she could not turn her thoughts away, not merely from Alvar, but from her life without him. Fain would she have refused the invitation which soon arrived to a solemn dinner party at Oakby; but it had been accompanied by a hint from Mr. Lester to her aunt which caused the latter to insist on accepting it, and they went accordingly to meet Sir John and Lady Hubbard, and one or two other neighbours. Mr. Lester was markedly polite to Virginia. Mrs. Lester wore her best black velvet, and a certain diamond brooch, only produced on occasions of state. Jack looked proper, silent, and bored. Every one wished to ask after the universally popular Cheriton, but felt that Alvar was an awkward subject of conversation, so that the adventures of the travellers could not be used to enliven the dulness. Nettie did not of course appear at dinner, and afterwards sat in a corner of the drawing-room in her white muslin, apparently determined not to open her mouth. Dick strolled up to her when the gentlemen came in, and was instantly followed by Jack, who stood by her silent and frowning.

Nettie looked up under her eyebrows, and said, " Dick, I am going to London."

" So I hear," said Dick, with a smile and a slight shrug.

" I hate it, but I can't help it. *You go on.*"

Dick smiled again and nodded, and then looked at Jack with an air of secret amusement, indescribably provoking. " All right," he said, but he turned away and made no further demonstration ; and Mrs. Lester desired Nettie to show Miss Hubbard " Views on the Rhine," a very handsome book reserved for occasions of unusual dulness.

Altogether the evening did not raise Virginia's spirits, and she was half inclined to resent the special kindness shown to her by Mr. Lester, as implying blame to his absent son.

It was a wonderful change of scene and circumstance, when she found herself, some few days later, sitting in Lady Charlton's pleasant London drawing-room, full of books, work, plants, and pretty things, with Ruth, bright-eyed and blooming, sitting on the rug at her feet, ready for a confidential chatter.

She was to be married directly after Christmas, she told Virginia. Rupert did not mean to sell out of the army; she did not at all dislike the notion of moving about for a few years, and now the regiment was at Aldershot she could see Rupert often while she remained in London to get her things.

" And, Queenie, you must choose the dresses for the bridesmaids. Grandmamma will have a gay wedding. *I* think it will be a great bore."

" Your bridesmaids ought to wear something warm and gay and bright, like yourself, Ruthie. Are you going to ask Nettie Lester ? "

" Oh, no ! " said Ruth hurriedly. " Why should I ? "

" She is Rupert's cousin, and she is so handsome."

" I never thought of her ! I am angry with them all since Don Alvar has made

you miserable. My darling Queenie, I
should like to stamp on him! Now, don't
be angry; but tell me how it all came
about?"

"I don't think I could ever make you
understand it, Ruth. He did nothing
wrong. It was only that—that I did not
suit him, and I found it out," said Virginia,
with a sort of ache in her voice, as she
turned her head away.

"The more—well, I won't finish the
sentence. Any way, he has spoiled your
life for you; for I am afraid he is *your*
love if you are not his," said Ruth, scan-
ning her sad face curiously. " Queenie,
weren't you ready to kill him and Cherry,
too, when they went off comfortably
together?"

"No," said Virginia, "he could not
help going—*that* was not it. And as for
Cherry, he was the only person who understood anything about it—he was so kind!
Oh, I hope he is really better!"

"I dare say he is, by this time," said
Ruth, rather oddly; "but they are all so

easily frightened about him—they spoil
him. I wonder what they would all say if
he fell in love with a naughty, wicked
siren—a female villain, who broke his heart
for him—just for fun."

" She would break something worth
having," said Virginia indignantly. " But,
do you know anything about Cherry,
Ruth ? "

" I ? I don't believe in sirens who break
hearts just for fun and vanity. And as
for Cherry, if he did meet with a little
trouble, he'd mend up again, heart and
lungs and all. There's something happy-
go-lucky about him—don't you think so ? "

" I think Cherry is too many-sided to be
left without an object in life, if that is what
you mean," said Virginia. " Besides, it is
so different for a man, they can always
do something."

Then Ruth put aside the little uneasy
feeling of self-reproach and doubt that had
prompted her to talk about Cherry, and
put her arms round Virginia, kissing her
tenderly.

" My darling Queenie ! You have been
fretting all by yourself at Elderthwaite till
things seem worse than they are."

" No," said Virginia ; " but my life has
all gone wrong. When I found that he
did not love me everything seemed over
for me."

Ruth interposed a question, and at last acquired a clearer knowledge of the circumstances under which Alvar and her cousin
had parted. She had a good deal of knowledge of the world, and some judgment,
though she did not always use it for her
own benefit, and she did not think that the
case sounded hopeless. She tried an ex-
periment.

" If you gave him up, Queenie, because
you discovered that he did not come up to
your notions of what he ought to be, why
there's an end of it, for he never will;
but it looks to me much more like a very
commonplace lovers' quarrel aggravated
by circumstances. He isn't a bad sort of
fellow in his own way; but it's not the
way that you think perfection."

" I did not quarrel with him, and I think the failure was in myself. Why should he love me ?—it does not seem as if I was very lovable."

There crossed Virginia's young gentle face a look that was like a foretaste of the bitterness and self-weariness that had seized on so many of her race—a sort of self-scorn that was not wholesome.

" Why should you think so ? " said Ruth.

" I think I should have got on better at home if I had been."

She spoke humbly enough, but there was utter discouragement in every line of her face and figure.

" Nonsense ! " said Ruth briskly. " Nobody would get on, in your sense, at Elderthwaite. I don't think you ought to stay there. You know it is quite in your power to arrange differently. You might make them long visits and—come fresh to every one."

" I'll never have it said that I could not live there," said Virginia, colouring

deeply. "And if I was away—I could not
—I would not—"

"Go back into the neighbourhood?
Well, at any rate you are going to have
a holiday now, and see something besides
moors and mud."

The change of scene could not fail to
do Virginia good, though there might be
something in the courtship of Ruth and
Rupert to remind her, with a difference,
of her own. It was sometimes breezy, for
Rupert loved to tease his betrothed, and
having got his will, was a free-and-easy
and contented lover, not much liking to be
put out of his way, and not quite coming
up to Ruth's requirements.

Ruth, though very kind to her cousin,
believed that she had lost her lover in
great measure through a feminine scrupu-
losity and desire to bring him up to her
own standard. Ruth would never be so
narrow and unsympathetic, *she* would be
prepared to understand *all* the story of her
hero's life; and being young, and much
more simple than she believed herself to

be, thought that her indiscriminate reading of somewhat free-spoken novels, gave her the necessary experience. But Rupert took quite another view. He was not aware of having any particular story to tell, and had no intention whatever of telling it. He did not in the least desire Ruth's sympathy with his past, which was quite common-place. He was not in a state of repentance, desirous of making a confession; nor had his heart ever been withered up. by any frightful experiences. No doubt he could remember much that was not particularly creditable, and which he rightly thought unfit for discussion with his betrothed. Moreover, he did not care at all for poetry, and very little for novels, and at last actually told her that one she mentioned was unfit for her to read.

Ruth was very angry, and had a sense of being put aside. Had Rupert—like her-self—a secret, or was she going to be "only a little dearer than his horse"? as she expressed it to herself, and with tears to him. Rupert laughed, and then grew a little angry, and then they made it up again; but he teased her for her romance, laughed at her most muscular and strong-souled heroes, and never would put himself in a heroic attitude. Ruth quarrelled with him, made it up with him, was vexed by him, and sometimes was vexatious; but all the while she never told him about Cheriton.

CHAPTER XXXII.

DON JUAN.

" I wonder if the spring-tide of this year
  Will bring another spring both lost and dear ;
  If heart and spirit will find out their spring,
  Or if the world *alone* will bud and sing."

IT was a bright sunny day in December,
fresh enough to make the Sevillanos pull
their picturesque cloaks over their shoulders out of doors, and light scraps of
wood-fire in their sitting-rooms, but with
the sun pouring down in unveiled splendour
over quaint painted relics of a bygone
world, when the Moor employed his rich
fancy in decorating the city, and over dark
Gothic arches and towers that seemed to
tell of a life almost equally remote from
nineteenth-century England. It was a
very new sort of Christmas weather for
Jack Lester as he tried to find his way

from the railway station to Don Guzman
de la Rosa's house. He soon discovered
that he had lost it, and stopped by a fruit-
stall piled with grapes, oranges, and melons
to ask the brown, skinny old woman in a
gay handkerchief who kept it, for some
directions, hoping that she would at least
understand the name of the street. So
she did, but it seemed to him that she
pointed in every direction at once, and
Jack stared round bewildered as a young
lady stepped across the street towards the
fruit-stall. Jack looked at her and she
looked full at him from under her straw
hat, with a pair of eyes dark as any in
Andalusia, but direct and clear, level and
fearless, as her face broke into a smile just
saved from a laugh.

"If you are looking for Don Guzman de
la Rosa's," she said in distinct and com-
prehensible English, "I can direct you;
but your brothers, Mr. Lester, are much
nearer, at my father's, Mr. Stanforth's.
Will you come there with me when I have
bought some fruit?"

"Oh, thank you immensely! I—I thought I would walk up, and I couldn't find the way. Thank you," said Jack, colouring and looking rather foolish.

" They did not expect you to be here till to-morrow. What have you done with your things ? "

" I've lost them, Miss Stanforth," said Jack; "I can't think how. You see no one understands anything, and the stations coming from Madrid are so odd."

" Oh, I think you will get them; we had one box detained for ages. Thank you," as he took her basket of fruit. " Shall we come ? " and then, looking up at him, " Your brother is so much better."

" I—I am very glad of that," said Jack, in a sort of inadequate way.

He was nervous about the meeting, and felt conscious that he was dusty with his journey, and sure that he must have looked foolish staring at the old woman.

Gipsy took him down the street, and into a house with a balcony covered with gay-striped blinds, and led him upstairs till she came to a door, or rather curtain, which she lifted, putting her finger on her lip.

It was a long, low room, with the lights carefully arranged and shaded, containing drawing-boards and unframed sketches, a wonderful heap of " art treasures," in one corner, Algerine scarves and stuffs, great, rough, green pitchers, and odds and ends of colour. Some one sat with his back to the door drawing, but Jack only beheld his brothers who were together at the further end of the room, and did not immediately see him, for they were looking at each other and appeared to the puzzled Jack oddly still and silent.

Miss Stanforth gave a little ¡laugh, and Alvar looked round and exclaimed. Cheriton sprang up, and with a cry of delight seized on Jack, with an outburst of greetings and inquiries, in which all the surroundings were forgotten. Gipsy laughingly described her encounter to Alvar; while " father," and " granny," " the old parson," " no good in having a Christmas at all at home without you," passed rapidly between the other two.

" Come, Jack, that's strong ! But, indeed, I think you have brought Christmas here. How rude we are ! You have never spoken to Mr. Stanforth. Mr. Stanforth, let him see the picture. Jack, do you think father will like it ? "

" Yes. You look much jollier than in the photograph," said Jack, as Mr. Stanforth turned the picture round for his inspection.

It was a small half-length in tinted chalk showing Cherry seated and looking up, with a bright interested face, at Alvar, who was showing him a branch of pomegranates. The execution was of the slightest, but the likenesses were good, and the strong contrast of colouring and resemblance of form was brought out well. " *Brothers*," was written underneath, and Jack looked at them as if the idea of any one wishing to make studies of them was strange to him.

" Jack is bewildered—lost, in more senses than one," said Cherry, smiling.

"Come, it is time we went home, and then
for news of every one! Mr. Stanforth, we
shall see you to-night."

Jack's arrival was an intense pleasure to
Cheriton, whose reviving faculties were
beginning to long for their old interests.
He had recovered his natural spirits, and
though he still looked delicate, and
had no strength to spare, was quite well
enough to look forward to his return to England and to beginning life there. Indeed
the ardent hopes and ambitions, so cruelly
checked in their first outlet, turned—with
a difference indeed, but with considerable
force—to the desire of distinction and
success; and in return for Jack's endless
talk of home and Oxford, he planned the
course of study to begin at Easter, and the
hard work which he felt sure with patience
must ensure good fortune. Cheriton was
very sanguine, and since he had felt so
much better, had no doubt of entire recovery;
and Jack was accustomed to follow his
lead, and was much relieved both by his
liveliness and by his resolute mention of

Rupert, and inquiry as to the arrangements for his marriage.

If Cheriton had not won the battle, he was at least holding his own in it bravely —the bitter pain was first submitted to, and then held down with a strong hand. But surely, he thought, there was *something* in store for him, if not the sweetness of happy love, yet the ardour of the struggle of life.

He could not say enough of Alvar's care for him, and Jack found Alvar much more easy of access than at home, and more interested than he had expected in the details of the home life; and in the course of conversation the dinner-party to the Seytons, and its motive, came out.

Alvar coloured deeply; he was silent then, but as soon as he was alone with Cheriton he said with some hurry of manner,—

"My brother, I am ashamed. What can I do? It is not endurable to me that any one should blame Miss Seyton."

"I suppose my father did the only thing

there was to be done. When an engagement is broken people generally say that there were faults on both sides."

"That is not so," said Alvar. "She is as blameless as a lily. Can I do nothing? I am ashamed," he repeated vehemently.

"Perhaps when you go home you will be able to show the world that you are of a different opinion," said Cherry very quietly, but with difficulty suppressing a smile.

"You do not understand," said Alvar in a tone of displeasure, turning away, and thinking that he had never before known Cheriton so unsympathetic.

Jack did not make much way with the de la Rosas, he did not like committing himself to foreign languages, and was shy, but they were very polite to "Don Juan," a name that so tickled Cheriton's fancy that he adopted it at once.

Jack began by somewhat resenting his brother's intimacy with the Stanforths as a strange and unnecessary novelty, but he soon fell under the charm, and pursued Mr. Stanforth with theories of art which

were received with plenty of good-humoured
banter. Gipsy, too, set to work to enlighten him on Spanish customs; and
having rescued him from one difficulty,
made it her business to show him the way
he should go, so that they became very
friendly, and the strange Christmas in this
foreign country drew the little party of
English closer together. There was
enough to interest them in the curious and
picturesque customs of Andalusia, ·but the
carols which Gipsy insisted on getting up
gave Cherry a fit of home-sickness; and a
great longing for Oakby, and the holly and
the snow, the familiar occupations, the
dogs, and the skating came over him. It
had been a long absence; he thought how
his father would be wishing for him, and
he experienced that sudden doubt of the
future which people call presentiment.
Would he ever spend Christmas *at home*
again? He was beginning to weary a little
of the wonder and admiration that had
stood him in such good stead, and to want
the time-honoured landmarks which showed

themselves unchanged as the flood-tide of passion subsided.

He was quite ready, however, to enter into the plans for a tour through some of the neighbouring towns before the Stanforths should return home at the end of January. Jack's time was still shorter; and as Cheriton himself had hitherto seen nothing but Seville, a joint expedition was proposed, with liberty to separate whenever it was convenient, as Alvar would consent to nothing that involved Cherry in long days on horseback lasting after sundown, or in extra rough living; and Mr. Stanforth backed up his prudent counsels.

But Cordova, Granada, and Malaga could be managed without any extreme fatigue, and Ronda could be reached easily from the latter place. So in the first week in the new year the three Lesters, Mr. Stanforth and his daughter, and Miss Weston set off together for a fortnight's trip. Afterwards they would all separate, and Alvar and Cheriton, after returning for a few weeks to Seville, were to make their

way gradually northwards, stopping in
France and Italy till the spring was further
advanced.

The tour prospered, and in due time
they found themselves at Ronda, and strolling out together in the lovely afternoon
sunshine, reached the new bridge across
the river; Jack and Gipsy engaged in an
endless discussion on the expulsion of the
Moors, lingering while they talked, and
looking down into the deep volcanic chasm
that divides the old town of Ronda from
the new, while nearly three hundred feet
below them roared, dashed, and sparkled
the silvery waters of the Guadalvin. On
either side were the picturesque buildings
of the two towns, fringed with wood—in
front, miles of orchards, and beyond, the
magnificent snow-crowned mountains of the
Sierra; while over all was the sapphire
blue, and sun, which, though the year was
but a fortnight old, covered the ground
with jonquils, and hung the woods with
lovely flowers hardly known to our hot-
houses.

They had marvelled at the Alhambra, and Cheriton had disclaimed all sense of feeling himself in the Crystal Palace. They had noticed and admired the mixture of Moorish and Christian art in Granada and Cordova, and had discussed ardently all the difficult questions of the Moorish occupation and expulsion—discussions in which Gipsy's fresh school knowledge, and Jack's ponderous theories, had met in many a hearty conflict. They had sketched, made notes, collected curiosities, or simply enjoyed the beauty according to their several idiosyncrasies, and had remained good friends through all the ups and downs of travel; while Cheriton had stood the fatigue so well that he had set his heart on riding with the others across country to Seville, and could afford to laugh at the discomforts incidental to eating and sleeping at Ronda. There was much to see there, and they did not mean to hurry away. Cherry remarked to Alvar that Jack had improved, and was less sententious than he used to be; but the cause of this increased geniality had struck no one. Every one laughed when Gipsy reminded him of things that he had forgotten, talked Spanish for him because he was too shy to commit himself to an unknown tongue, and stoutly contradicted many of his favourite sentiments. Writing an essay, was he? on the evil of regarding everything from a ludicrous point of view. There were a great many cases in which that was the best point of view to look at things, and Gipsy wrote a counter essay which afforded great amusement. But no one perceived when Gipsy's sense of the ludicrous fell a little into abeyance; and when she ceased to contradict Jack flatly, and began to think that she received new ideas from him, still less did his brothers dream of the new thoughts and aspirations that were rushing confusedly through the boy's mind; he was hardly conscious of them himself.

The pair were a little ahead of their companions, who now came up and joined them.

"Well, Jack," said Alvar, "I have been making inquiries, and I find that we can take the excursion among the mountains that you wished for. Mr. Stanforth prefers making sketches here, and it would be too rough for the ladies, or for Cherry."

"I suppose the mountains *are* very fine?" said Jack, not very energetically.

" Jack found the four hundred Moorish steps too much for him. He has grown lazy," said Cherry. " For my part, I think the fruit market is the nicest place here ; it has such a splendid view. I shall go there to-morrow and eat melons while you are away."

" Miss Weston and I are going to buy scarves and curiosities in the market," said Gipsy ; " but they say we should have come here in May to see the great fair ; that is the time to buy beautiful things."

" Yes," said Alvar, " and Mr. Stanforth might have studied all the costumes of Andalusia. But, I think, since we ordered our dinner two hours ago, it is likely now to be ready. I hope the ladies are not tired of fried pork, for I do not think we shall get anything better."

"Oh!" said Gipsy, "I mean to get mamma to introduce it at home; it is so good."

"Do you, my dear?" said her father. "I am inclined to think that with the ordinary accompaniments of clean table-cloths and silver forks it might be disappointing."

Without a table-cloth and with the very primitive implements of Ronda, the fried pork was very welcome; and when their dinner was over, as it was too dark to go out any more, they went down into the great public room on the ground floor of the inn, where round a bright wood fire were gathered muleteers, other travellers and natives, both men and women.

It was a wonderful picturesque scene in the light of the fire, and Mr. Stanforth's sketching so delighted his subjects that they crowded round him, only anxious that he should draw them all, while the "English hidalgos" were objects of the greatest curiosity. The men came up to Jack and Cheriton, examining their clothes, their

tobacco pouches and pipes; and one great
fellow in a high hat, and brilliant-coloured
shirt, looking so much like an ideal brigand
that it was difficult to believe that he was
only an olive-grower, after looking at Cheriton for some time, put out a very dirty
hand, and touched his hair and cheek as if
to assure himself that they were of the
same substance as his own. Gipsy's dress
and demeanour interested them greatly,
and one or two of them made her write her
name on a bit of paper for them to keep.

The next day's ride was fully discussed,
and much information given as to route and
destination. Then, at Cherry's request,
some of the muleteers sang to them wild
half-melancholy airs, and one of the men
danced a species of comic dance for their
edification, and then the chief musician
diffidently requested them to give a specimen of *their* national music. Gipsy laughed
and looked shy; but her father laid down
his pencil, and in a· fine voice, and with
feeling that told even in an unknown
language, sang "Tom Bowling," and then,

as this gave great satisfaction, began
" D'ye ken John Peel," in the chorus of
which his companions joined him.

" That," he explained, " was a hunting
song. Now he would give them a really
national air;" and in the midst of this
strange audience, he struck up the familiar
notes of " God save the Queen."

The English rose to their feet; the men
lifted their hats, and all joined in and
sang the old words with more patriotic
fervour than at home they might have
thought themselves capable of; and the
Spaniards, with quick wit and ready
courtesy, uncovered also, and when they
had finished the musician picked out the
notes on his guitar.

The weather next morning proving all
that could be wished, Alvar and Jack, with
a couple of guides, set off before daybreak
on their ride into the mountains, intending
to ascend on foot a certain peak from which
the view was very fine, and which was
accessible in the winter. The expedition
had been entirely planned for Jack's benefit,

and perhaps he was not quite so grateful
as he might have been. The others had
no lack of occupation. They went down
to the " Nereid's Grotto," a cave filled with
clear emerald water, near which stand an
old Moorish mill, built on rocks, fringed
with masses of maidenhair fern. Mr. Stanforth remained there sketching the building,
white with a sort of dazzling eastern
whiteness, the strange forms of cactus and
aloe crowning the cliffs, and the washer-
women in gay handkerchiefs and scarlet
petticoats kneeling on the flat stones by
the river. Cheriton, with the ladies, went
on their shopping expedition to find pre-
sents that might be sent home by Jack, and
having found some silk handkerchiefs for
his father, a wonderful sash for Nettie, and
a striped rug for his grandmother, to whom
Alvar intended to despatch some Spanish
lace already bought in Seville,· he helped
Gipsy to choose a present for each of her
numerous brothers and sisters, and himself
hunted up smaller offerings for his friends
of all degrees.

This occupied a long time, especially as the children followed them wherever they went, "as if one was the pied piper," said Cherry; and afterwards they bought bread and fruit, and ate it for luncheon, and Gipsy reflected that in three weeks' time she would be back in Kensington, very busy and rather gay, and would probably never buy pomegranates and melons in Ronda again in all her life.

Cheriton employed himself in the evening in writing to his father, while the Stanforths went down again to the mixed company below. He did not expect his brothers till late, and was not giving much heed to the time, when he looked up and saw Gipsy cross the room.

"Have they come back?" he said.

"No," said Gipsy. "Don't you think they ought to be here soon?"

Cherry glanced at his watch.

"Nine o'clock? Yes, I suppose they will be here directly, for the guides told us eight. People never get off mountains as soon as they expect they will.

I'll come down. I have finished my letter."

Some time longer passed without any sign of an arrival, and the landlord of the inn, and some of the muleteers, began to say that either the Ingleses must have changed their route, or that something must have detained them till it was too dark to get down the mountains, so that they must be waiting till daylight to descend. Cheriton did not take alarm quickly; he knew that a very trifling change of path or weather would make this possible, and he was the first to say that they had better go to bed, and expect to see the wanderers in the morning; and Mr. Stanforth, very anxious to avoid frightening him, chimed in with a cheerful augury to the same effect. But when Cheriton had left them, he said, anxiously,—

" I don't like it ; I am sure Alvar would not delay if he could help it—he would not cause so much anxiety."

"But some very trifling matter might

s 2

have detained them till after dark," said Miss Weston.

" Oh, yes; I trust it may be so."

Gipsy said nothing; but before her mind's eye there rose a vision of more than one little wayside cross which she had been shown on their ride to Ronda, with the inscription, " Here died Don Luis or Don Pedro," and the date.

These were erected, she was told, where travellers had been killed by *saltiadores* or brigands; but there were very few of such breakers of the law in Andalusia now. Still, their party had thought it right to carry arms. What if they had been driven to use them ?—what if—? Even to herself Gipsy could not finish the sentence; but she lay awake all night listening for an arrival, till her ears ached and burnt with the strain ; till she heard in the night-time, that had hitherto seemed to her so silent, sounds innumerable; till she felt as if she could have heard their footsteps on the mountain side. And all the time the worst of it was that she heard nothing. And for fear that Miss Weston would guess at her terror, for speaking of it seemed to remove it from the vague regions of her imagination and give it new force, and also for fear of missing a sound, she lay as still as a mouse, till, spite of an occasional doze, the night seemed endless, and the most welcome thing in the world was the long-delayed winter dawn.

Gipsy was thankful to get up and dress and find out what was going on, and as soon as possible she ran downstairs and went out to the front of the inn. Her father was just before her, and Cheriton was standing talking to a group of guides and muleteers. He turned round and came up to them saying,—

" I have been making inquiries, and they say that if they kept to their intended route—and I feel sure that they would not change it—there is no reason to fear any dangerous accident such as one hears of on Swiss mountains. And the men all laugh at the notion of any brigandage nowadays. What I think is, that one of them may have got some slight hurt, twisted his foot, for instance, and been unable to get on; and if they don't turn up in an hour or so I think we ought to go after them."

Cherry looked anxiously at Mr. Stanforth as he spoke, as if, having worked up this view for his own benefit, he wanted to see others convinced by it also.

" Yes," said Mr. Stanforth, " I have been thinking of the possibility of strained ankles too."

" You see," said Cherry, " they must have left their mules somewhere; at least we shall fall in with them."

" Ah—ah! they are coming," cried Gipsy, with a scream of joy, as the sound of hoofs were heard along the street.

Cherry dashed forward, but as the party came into sight he stopped suddenly, then hurried on to meet them; for only Pedro, one of the mule-drivers who had accompanied them, appeared, riding one mule and leading the other.

In the sudden downfall, Gipsy's very senses seemed to fail her; as she saw

Cherry lay his hand on the mule as if to support himself, and look up, unable to frame a question; she could hardly hear the confusion of voices that followed.

Soon, however, she gathered that no terrible news had come—no news at all. Don Alvar and Don Juan had ascended the mountain with their guide José, and had never returned; and, after waiting for their descent in the early morning, Pedro had come back without them. What could have happened? *They might* have gone a long way round, in fact a three days' route—there was no other, or they might have fallen from a precipice.

· "In short, you know nothing about them. We must go and see," interrupted Cherry, briefly; "at least, I will. What mules have you? Who is the best guide now in Ronda?"

"My dear boy," said Mr. Stanforth gently and reluctantly, "you must not try the mountain yourself. You know it must be done on foot, and the fatigue—"

"How can I think of that now? What

does it matter?" said Cherry, with the roughness of excessive pain. "It is far worse to wait."

"Yes, but depend upon it, *they* are as anxious as you are. Certainly I shall go, and the guides; but, you see, speed is an object."

"Oh, I shouldn't cough and lose my breath *now!*" said Cherry. "Indeed, I can walk up hill."

Mr. Stanforth could hardly answer him, and he went on vehemently,—

"You know Alvar is much too fidgety; he thinks I can do nothing. But, at least, let us all ride to the foot of the mountain; perhaps we shall meet them yet."

"Yes, that at any rate we will do. Give your orders, and then come and get some chocolate."

Miss Weston had taken care that this was ready, and Cherry sat down and ate and drank, trying to put a good face on the matter before the ladies.

After they started on their ride he was

very silent, and hardly spoke a word till they came to the little inn where the mules had been left the day before. Then he said very quietly to Mr. Stanforth,—

"Perhaps I had better wait—I might hinder you."

"I think it would be best," said Mr. Stanforth, with merciful absence of comment, for he knew what the sense of incapacity must have been to Cherry then.

The kindest thing was to start on the steep ascent at once. Miss Weston, in what Gipsy thought a cold-blooded manner, took out her drawing materials, and sat down to sketch the mountain peaks, Cheriton started from his silent watch of the ascending party, and asked Gipsy to take a little walk with him : and as she gladly came, they gathered plants and talked a little about the view, showing their terror by their utter silence on the real object of their thoughts. Then he exerted himself to get some lunch for them; so that the first hours of the day passed pretty well. But as the afternoon wore on, he sat down under a great walnut-tree, and watched the mountain—the great pitiless creature with its steep bare sides and snowy summits. He gave no outward sign of impatience, only watched as if he could not turn his eyes away; and Miss Weston, almost as anxious for him as for the missing ones, thought it best to leave him to follow his own bent.

No one was anxious about poor Gipsy, who wandered about, running out of sight in the vain hope of seeing something on the bare hill-side on her return.

At last, just as the wonderful violet and rose tints of the sunset began to colour the white peaks, Cheriton sprang to his feet, and pointed to the hill-side, where, far in the distance, were moving figures.

" How many ? " he said, for, in the hurry of their start, they had left the field-glasses, which would have brought certainty a little sooner, behind.

" Oh, there are surely a great many," said Gipsy.

Cheriton watched with the keen sight

trained on his native moorlands; while
the ladies counted and miscounted, and
thought they saw Jack's white puggery.

" No," said Cherry, " there are only Mr.
Stanforth and the two guides. I *cannot*
wait," he added, impetuously, and began
to hurry up the hill, till he stopped per-
force for want of breath.

" There can have been no accident ; we
have found no one—nothing whatever,"
cried Mr. Stanforth, as soon as he came
within speaking distance. " They must
have gone the other way; there is no
trace."

He spoke in a tone of would-be congra-
tulation, but an ominous whisper passed
among the guides, *bandidas*, and the utter
blank was almost more terrifying than
direct ill news.

" We must go back to Ronda, and see
what can be done to-morrow."

" But," said Cherry, rather incoherently,
" I don't know—you see, I must take
care of Jack."

" Yes," said Mr. Stanforth, " but any

little detention would not hurt either of
them, and they must not find that you are
knocked up. We can consult the authorities at Ronda."

" Yes, thank you; I hope you are not
over-tired," said Cherry, half dreamily.
" I ? oh, no; I am quite well; but I can't
help being anxious."

" No, it is very perplexing; but I feel
quite hopeful of good news myself," said
Mr. Stanforth.

But somehow the necessity of this assurance struck a sharper pang to Cherry's
heart than his own vague forebodings.

END OF VOL. II.

GILBERT AND RIVINGTON, PRINTERS, ST. JOHN'S SQUARE, LONDON.

www.ingramcontent.com/pod-product-compliance
Lightning Source LLC
Chambersburg PA
CBHW060614030726
47498CB00005B/1676